THE FLYING BOAT MYSTERY

Paul Halter books from Locked Room International:
The Lord of Misrule (2010)
The Fourth Door (2011)
The Seven Wonders of Crime (2011)
The Demon of Dartmoor (2012)
The Seventh Hypothesis (2012)
The Tiger's Head (2013)
The Crimson Fog (2013)
The Night of the Wolf (2013) (collection)
The Invisible Circle (2014)
The Picture from the Past (2014)
The Phantom Passage (2015)
Death Invites You (2016)
The Vampire Tree (2016)
The Madman's Room (2017)
The Man Who Loved Clouds (2018)
The Gold Watch (2019)

Other impossible crime novels from Locked Room International:
The Riddle of Monte Verita (Jean-Paul Torok) 2012
The Killing Needle (Henry Cauvin) 2014
The Derek Smith Omnibus (Derek Smith) 2014
The House That Kills (Noel Vindry) 2015
The Decagon House Murders (Yukito Ayatsuji) 2015
Hard Cheese (Ulf Durling) 2015
The Moai Island Puzzle (Alice Arisugawa) 2016
The Howling Beast (Noel Vindry) 2016
Death in the Dark (Stacey Bishop) 2017
The Ginza Ghost (Keikichi Osaka) 2017
Death in the House of Rain (Szu-Yen Lin) 2017
The Double Alibi (Noel Vindry) 2018
The 8 Mansion Murders (Takemaru Abiko) 2018
Locked Room Murders (Robert Adey) 2018 (bibliography)
The Seventh Guest (Gaston Boca) 2018

Visit our website at www.mylri.com or
www.lockedroominternational.com

THE FLYING BOAT MYSTERY

FRANCO VAILATI

Translated by Igor Longo

The Flying Boat Mystery

This book is a work of fiction. The characters, incidents, and dialogue are drawn from the author's imagination and are not to be construed as real. Any resemblance to actual events or persons, living or dead, is entirely coincidental.

First published in Italian in 1935 by
I Libri Gialli as *Il mistero dell'idrovolante*
Copyright © Arnoldo Mondadori Editore S.p.A., Milano, 1935.
THE FLYING BOAT MYSTERY
English translation copyright © by John Pugmire 2019.

All rights reserved. No part of this book may be used or reproduced in any manner whatsoever without written permission except in the case of brief quotations embodied in critical articles and reviews.

Every effort has been made to trace the holders of copyright. In the event of any inadvertent transgression of copyright, the editor would like to hear from the author's representatives. Please contact me at pugmire1@ yahoo.com.

FIRST AMERICAN EDITION
Library of Congress Cataloguing-in-Publication Data
Vailati, Franco
[*Il mistero dell'idrovolante* English]
The Flying Boat Mystery / Franco Vailati
Translated from the Italian by Igor Longo

To Igor, who patiently provided this translation. J.M.P

PRINCIPAL CHARACTERS

Passengers on the Do-Wal 134:

GIORGIO VALLESI Journalist
FRANCESCO AGLIATI Banker
MARCELLA ARTENI
GIUSEPPI SABELLI Merchant
GIOVANNI MARCHETTI Merchant
PAGELLI-BERTIERI Merchant
LARINI Teller
VANNA SANDRELLI
MARIA MARTELLI
AUGUSTO MARTELLI

Crew:

COMANDANTE GIRINI Flight Commander
SECONDO PILOTA VANDELLI Second Pilot

Police:

VICE QUESTORE LUIGI RENZI Assistant Commissioner
COMMENDATORE BERTINI Commissioner
COMMISSARIO BOLDRIN Chief Inspector
VICE COMMISSARIO GALBIATI Superintendent

1-OSTIA-NAPLES

The landscape around the Ostia airport was mournfully tedious and flat. The mouth of the Tiber river was a bilge-yellow strip in the sandy coastline. The water slumbered under the sky's disinterested grey eye. Even the sea had a neutral tint, as if it were ashamed of showing off a glossy, festive blue in the general greyness of the surroundings. A casual whisper of air barely disturbed the wide wings of the flying boats resting within the protective arms of the airport's small water basins.

They were all dominated by their powerful big brother, the Dornier-Wal 134, the new-fangled flying boat connecting Rome to Palermo, which had entered into service after a massive advertising campaign to laud its comfort and technical perfection, which had allowed the titanic plane to rival the best foreign models. About twenty people surrounded it: mechanics, airport clerks, passengers arriving from Rome on the airline bus. No one would endure the arduous five-kilometre trip along the Rome-Ostia highway to the isolated airport out of idle curiosity.

The departure was scheduled for quarter-past-eleven, and the plane was ready to go. The porters were filling the luggage compartment in the tail, and almost all the passenger seats were already occupied. Only one place was still empty. A green booking card satisfied the curiosity of the other passengers, announcing proudly that it was reserved for banker Francesco Agliati from Ostia to Naples.

Suddenly a car honked from the access road. A green cab raced across the asphalt and its brakes screeched as it came to a sudden stop outside the large glass walls of the Airport Terminal. Its passenger emerged and ran anxiously towards the check-in desk:

'At what time does the plane for Palermo leave?'

'At quarter-past-eleven, sir.'

'May I have a ticket for....'

'I'm sorry, sir. The plane is full.'

The man tried to wipe the sweat from his balding forehead. His grizzled moustache twitched:

'Full? But that's impossible....'

'The plane is full,' repeated the clerk patiently.

'But I must absolutely be in Palermo before nightfall.'

The unfortunate passenger gripped his briefcase anxiously.

'I'm sorry, sir, there is not a single place on the plane.' The clerk shrugged ironically. 'If you want to check it for yourself...' He indicated with an almost imperceptible movement of his head the grey bulk of the plane visible through the glass window.

After a brief moment of incertitude, the passenger capitulated and made a miserable exit from the Terminal Building. He started to wander around one of the little basins, but was stopped by a voice:

'Not here, sir! If you want to board, the plane stairway is on the right.' The round face of a mechanic in blue overalls appeared from behind the plane's tail.

The passenger circled around the plane, hoping to have found a secret helper:

'Please, they told me that there is no place on the plane...'

'Yes, we're full. Do you have a ticket?'

'I couldn't buy one, but if you would be so kind...'

The mechanic made the gesture of taking off his cap as he waited in silence for further explanation, whilst his fingers twitched nervously, as if he was still adjusting some delicate instrument.

'I must absolutely be in Palermo before dusk. I'm ready to travel with the luggage, sitting on my briefcase... Of course, my friend, I will....'

'Well, I could perhaps travel in the tail compartment myself, and you could occupy my seat in the cockpit, sir, but....'

The hopeful passenger was ready to brush off his remaining doubts. Several banknotes passed swiftly from one hand to another. Overwhelmed by the strong-willed and very persuasive anxiety of the generous passenger, the mechanic still feigned some token resistance and nodded towards the terminal offices:

'I must still talk to the pilots before....'

The mechanics were giving the propellers their first spin. After some jumps, the rhythm of the cylinders became regular and the motor sprang into life. Just as in a slapstick movie, at the very moment the ramp was being detached, a sleek limousine screeched to a halt and a fat little man got out, his hat crammed down over his grizzled head. After frantically asking that the ramp be put back into place, he ran up and into the cabin, waving his blue ticket under the nose of the attendant. Once inside, he distributed *pardons* to left and right in a more dignified manner, before eventually occupying the last remaining seat.

Reporter Giorgio Vallesi thought that he seemed more like a fat boy arriving out of breath at the dinner table, red-faced and ashamed for his lateness, than a big financier. Of course, Vallesi had at least a professional excuse for his own interest in the arrival of the powerful banker Francesco Agliati, given his previous attentive perusal of everybody else's green booking card.

But journalism was not really the passion of young Vallesi's life. Having studied politics and completely failing in his triumphal access to a diplomatic career, he had been constrained to accept a less ambitious role in the Commercial Bank. The barbed wires of numbers and strict working hours had been unable to constrain their grudging prisoner for more than six months, he having only too recently abandoned the happy life of the madcap, lazy college student, passing every day with friends at the Sapienza University students' club, or in a café or fashionable *perfumer salon*. His foremost hobby during that joyful period of his life was wasting time at street stands haggling endlessly and peevishly over the price of ties he had not the slightest intention of buying, for the sole purpose of enraging the duped merchants.

The newspaper was certainly an improvement. The work was sufficiently irregular to satisfy even his own difficult tastes, and his easy-going ways had always helped him in the most critical moments. Now, he was going to Palermo for an historical public celebration of a centennial anniversary of some sort. He had been allowed to travel by plane to write a colourful article for the paper, although the editor-in - chief had warned him that the public was beginning to be quite bored by colourful items about plane trips, in which reporters could very easily transform even a Roma-Frascati route into twenty-thousand words of picturesque impressions, and did so almost weekly.

The plane was effectuating the take-off manoeuvre. The mechanics had pushed the Dornier out of the basin, pointing it toward the barely perceivable sea current. The propellers were now in full action and the body of the plane bounced more and more swiftly on the water. After a minute of such breath-taking motion, Vallesi could suddenly see the bilge-yellow Tiber River below him. He was stunned for a moment at this sudden detachment from the safety of the Earth, which reminded him of a moment in his childhood when he tried to follow in astonished awe the slow and mysterious movement of the hands on his father's watch.

After two very wide spiral turns, the plane slowly began its regular flight. Below, the crowded Ostia beach swiftly became merely a smooth inclined plane down which the garish stains of the sunbathers seemed to slip in a precarious, toppling balance towards the grey sea, below the rock-solid borderline of the beach cabins.

Rome was only an undistinguished fleck ,the almost invisible goal of the small, spidery cars travelling swiftly with small, jerking movements on the grey highway. On the horizon, the cotton clouds were softening the usually sharp silhouette of the Latian hills. Isolated and neatly-shaped Monte Calvo was showing off its peculiar topside tonsure of trees, giving at a distance the false impression of the crenellated tower of a castle.

The reporter watched his fellow passengers with curiosity; apparently they had all brilliantly sustained their first contact with the sky, with only an occasional disgruntled comment about the sudden air-pockets. Even Agliati the banker... But why was the fascinating woman in red seated in front of him staring so intently at the powerful financier? Clearly Agliati had noticed her, and, highly embarrassed, was trying to bury himself in the mass of papers, dossiers and documents he kept in his bulky and official-looking briefcase.

The reporter looked with more attentive curiosity at the woman in red. Some years before, she would certainly have been a beautiful woman. Now her elegant figure was a bit too solid, and her cheeks were beginning to be puffy. Whilst her eyes showed a casual indifference, her body was a bundle of nerves and fears. Her head moved constantly from left to right, almost as if she feared the assault of a silent, tiptoeing adversary. Vallesi was a fashion expert, and he noticed a detail which might have escaped many a careless observer. On her elegantly clad knees, wrapped in a dark red silken tissue, she had placed a lizard-green bag which clashed horrendously. A lady dressed by Ventura would never have committed such a mortal sin of bad taste. Giorgio's great friend, the great hope of the Italian police,

Rome Assistant Commissioner Luigi Renzi, would have immediately deduced that the woman in red had been in too much of a rush to catch the plane to notice her own attire—and in a woman this was a classic clue of excitement, distress and possibly fear.

Giorgio felt very pleased with his own shrewd deductions. As a prize, he conceded himself the umpteenth look at the young woman in the seat to his right, by the name of Marcella Arteni. And, quite frankly, had we ourselves been on the plane, we would undoubtedly have followed his example.

Signorina Arteni was tall and slender, with shapely legs and a great harmony of figure, her lovely face enhanced by the golden tiara of her blonde hair. The simple blue-sky dress she was wearing was offset by a touch of eccentricity: a round and slightly lopsided straw hat. The soft, tender rouge of her lips was a real masterpiece, a perfect match for her rosy cheeks. Her lips made Giorgio remember with an ironic nostalgia the day he had boasted that he would never have to pay the celibacy tax (a tax imposed by Fascism with the objective of encouraging marriage and Italian repopulation, after the major exodus of the late nineteenth century).

Suddenly, the woman in red whispered something so softly that Vallesi was obliged to ask her to repeat the question:

'We're expected to arrive in Palermo before four o'clock, aren't we?'

'At half-past three, madam.'

The woman nodded as if the news had confirmed a secret thought, then began to stare again at the banker with her hazel eyes. But Agliati hadn't noticed her. Behind his glasses he was staring at something, without paying the least attention to the official business documents his grey-gloved hands were clutching.

Was it possible that he was sneaking an anxious glance at the three men towards the rear of the cabin? To a Roman's eye they had the unmistakable look of three Latian country tradesmen coming to town: large, swarthy faces; bristled moustaches; sturdy, squat figures; garish violet and dark brown suits stretched tightly. Two of them were old friends, whilst the third one was a more recent acquaintance. One of them, Giuseppe Sabelli by name, was leaving his seat. The enquiring eyes of his fellow passengers instinctively followed his progression along the narrow aisle between the seats. Vallesi could swear that the curiosity was far more sharp and intense in the banker's eyes than in the other passengers' eyes. Sabelli vanished behind the railway-wagon-like glass door which gave access to a small vestibule with the plane's exit door on the left, the small wooden door of the toilet on the right, and the glass cockpit door straight ahead.

When the country tradesman returned, he again attracted the instinctive curiosity of his fellow passengers, but the banker barely lifted his head. Possibly he wasn't really interested in the moustached triplet of Latian country merchants. And he was certainly not looking at the humble middle-class, middle-aged couple so cautiously enclosed in their protective shell. More likely he was staring at the man displaying the classic aloofness of the political class, who hardly addressed a single word to the two young minions placed protectively in his regal vicinity, from which vantage point they could cast ecstatic glances at the ravishing Marcella Arteni and forget about their own stomachs' grumbling protests against the plane's sudden jolts.

The silence in the cabin was only broken by the rustle of the small map given by the airline to its passengers, with the aid of which Signorina Arteni was following the plane's route with interest.

Giorgio hoped that she wouldn't leave the plane in Naples. In any case, he decided to swiftly make her acquaintance. After a brief misstep on the slick wooden aisle between the seats, he directed himself towards the glass door in the front. When he returned to the cabin, he announced in loud, booming voice:

'Ladies and gentlemen, I announce to you that we have a clandestine passenger on board!'

Twenty-two eyes looked with quizzical astonishment at the jovial reporter, but he noticed only the pair belonging to Marcella Arteni. His sudden trick seemed to have had a promising success, so he continued:

'He arrived at the last moment, and although the plane was full, he was somehow able to obtain the mechanic's place in the cockpit. Being quite a large man, I hope that his weight doesn't prove dangerous for the flight.'

Giorgio's joke was a sort of trial balloon, and a very silly one ,of course, but in certain cases silliness can be highly rewarding... He hadn't the slightest interest in the other passengers' reactions, but when Marcella Arteni looked at him with a sort of pitying amusement, in a compassionate effort to comfort him for his own blunder, it was not a promising start to a relationship.

Agliati, on the other hand, was clearly not at ease, and he decided suddenly to retire his large, bulky figure into the small toilet. As the passengers turned their attention again to poor Giorgio Vallesi, one of the country tradesmen called out:

'And the mechanic? Where is he?'

The reporter indicated the rear of the plane:

'The poor fellow has been exiled to the luggage compartment, and can probably hear what I'm saying, which, I must admit, is terribly indiscreet.'

Things were going much better now. The young lady had closed her eyes for a moment and was trying her best to suppress a smile of amusement. Noticing this promising reaction, Vallesi advanced cautiously towards her seat, whilst trying to think of something interesting to say:

'And so, we've had the chance to add a new and refreshing anecdote to our otherwise tedious trip....'

Giorgio was mildly irritated with himself for his timid approach to the girl, but he couldn't think of anything more exciting to say:

'Is this your first flight, Signorina...?'

'Yes, but who...? '

'I'm sorry to introduce myself like this. It's not a very correct thing to do, I know, but when you're floating in mid-air, conventions lose their grip... My name's Giorgio Vallesi.'

'Marcella Arteni, nice to meet you.'

Swift answer. Very curt smile, followed by a small pause—one of those little, frail dams of silence demanding to be impetuously broken:

'Don't be so serious, please.'

'Why?'

'You have a marvellous smile, don't be afraid of wearing it out.'

Marcella looked at him in astonishment at his impertinence and reacted by withdrawing into herself. But Vallesi continued his desperate attack:

'So, I'm trying to find some ridiculously funny remark in the hope of having the lucky chance to see it again. Good, now I can die happy.'

Marcella really had smiled. Possibly the young man was not too unpleasant after all. He was daring and very impertinent, yes, but at the same time he seemed to be praying for her to not be put off by it.

Vallesi was quite good-looking, after all, with his long, lean, boyish face. Quite a refined young man, daring but in some ways embarrassed by his own impertinence. His rosy cheeks perfectly matched his smooth, brown hair. Signorina Arteni looked out of the window. To her left, the grey mass of Mount Circeo loomed like a genial, saturnine big brother to the distant brown tooth of Torre Astura.

The blue-clad mechanic came out of the luggage compartment, massaging his knees and shoulders.

'Luggage doesn't travel in very comfortable places, does it?' asked the impertinent reporter.

The man in blue indicated the front of the plane:

'Ah, the one-hundred lire notes were very beautiful, but I'll never do it again! Luckily, we'll soon be in Naples and it will all be over!'

He went to join the pilots in the cockpit for a few minutes, possibly to repeat his comments to the clandestine passenger, and returned to the cabin carrying a yellow-paper parcel.

Gaeta Gulf was now behind them and the plane was flying over the small Pozzuoli Point. The landscape attracted curious passengers to the windows. It was quite a remarkable novelty to see beneath them the brown-blue film of the sea contrasting with the red-roofed coastline houses hidden amongst the trees.

Nobody noticed the nervous excitement of the second country tradesman, who was trying for the second time to open the locked toilet. After a third attempt he exploded in his gruff, coarse voice:

'Bloody hell, what's he doing in there? He's been inside for almost half an hour!'

His vulgar outburst seemed to upset his fellow passengers. The lady in red sat bolt upright:

'What's happening?'

In a gentler tone, the tradesman indicated the banker's empty seat:

'That fellow has been locked in the toilet for a long time....'

'The banker is still in there? Perhaps he's not feeling...,' interrupted Vallesi.

'The banker? What banker?' asked Marcella Arteni with an air of excitement.

The mechanic's face appeared from his den, curious. Hearing of the banker's strange absence, he seemed more surprised than worried:

'We must call the comandante immediately....'

The plane was descending swiftly, circling over the crowded port located inside the protruding white tongue of Beverello Wharf. Flight Commander Girini left the sea-landing manoeuvre to the second pilot, knocked on the toilet's small wooden door, called out Agliati's name, and pushed vigorously on the door twice. Not receiving any answer, he announced very calmly to the passengers:

'Please do not move after the landing. I and my crew will take care of the matter.'

The plane caressed the water at one-hundred km/h, and broke the surface, creating a wave like the wake of a departing steamship, which jolted it briefly. As the sea receded and the plane reduced speed, Commander Girini repeated his order to the passengers:

'Please do not leave your seats.'

Even before the gangways were firmly attached to the plane, the pilot was already running along the floating wharf. He quickly notified the airport commander of the incident, whilst his crew politely but firmly thwarted any attempt to leave the cabin. The clandestine passenger was no luckier than anybody else and was swiftly and firmly restrained in the cockpit. The police inspector on duty at Beverello Wharf arrived with two officers whilst two mechanics started to break down the toilet's small wooden door. The astonished passengers watched the operation from the cabin with curious apprehension. Attracted by the commotion, airport clerks and sailors from nearby ships were beginning to crowd around the front of the plane.

The two policemen took over from the mechanics, and the sudden surrender of the small door almost upset their precarious balance.

The toilet was empty.

Banker Francesco Agliati had vanished into thin air.

2-COMMISSARIO BOLDRIN

Assistant commissioner Luigi Renzi cut swiftly through the network of streets extending from the Tiber River to Monte Mario: Via dei Gracchi, Via degli Scipioni, Via Marcantonio Colonna, Via Fabio Massimo, Via Ottaviano... When he passed through that particular part of Rome, it always reminded him of his cousin, the mathematics professor, running to the University whilst tracing in his fertile mind fantastic, outlandish theorems about the right angles of the very straight and geometric Turin avenues.

A newsstand attendant shouted, advertising his wares :

'Italia! *La Tribuna* fifth edition! *Il Littoriale*! Special Tour De France edition! Pesenti beats Faure and Camusso on the Pyrenees with a breathtaking sprint!'

Luigi Renzi bought *La Tribuna* and *Il Littoriale*, happy about the Italian cyclist's swift assault on the Tour De France Yellow Shirt. But it was whilst he was quickly perusing *La Tribuna* that an article in the police news on the fourth page attracted his professional attention:

BANKER FRANCESCO AGLIATI VANISHES MYSTERIOUSLY FROM THE ROME-NAPLES PLANE

Almost immediately the Tour De France lost its alluring attraction. Unfortunately, the Naples correspondent was not forthcoming with very many details:

A mysterious disappearance happened today on the Ostia-Naples-Palermo SANA (Società Anonima Navigazione Aerea) flying boat. The new-fangled Dornier Do-Wal 134, now on its first flights, was carrying twelve passengers, amongst them the well-known banker Francesco Agliati, who boarded at Ostia. The flight was uneventful until the arrival just before Naples, when passengers were alarmed by the prolonged absence of the banker, who had entered the small toilet half an hour earlier. The door was locked from the inside and nobody responded to repeated calls. When the plane landed at Beverello

Wharf, the door was broken down, but the banker wasn't inside, despite all the passengers having seen him enter the toilet. Nevertheless, Agliati was no longer on the plane, and the subsequent search proved fruitless. No one could have entered the small locked room after the banker, so this mysterious and totally incongruous disappearance has, for the moment, no possible explanation. Hopefully, further questioning of passengers and crewmen will shed some light on the matter. Having noted personally Agliati's disappearance, Commissario Boldrin, on duty at the time in the Beverello Wharf Airport, has begun his investigation, but, up to the present, nothing has been revealed to the press.

Actually, the Naples police had followed the investigation with a certain anxiety. Chief Inspector Boldrin was a good man, but more suited to a small village constabulary in his native Veneto than to a big town. He had immediately been submitted to the assault of the passengers, upset by the delay caused by the mysterious incident. Only the important politician, a Foreign Office bigwig, was spared the consequences of the disaster. He was the first to be interrogated, and provided the police with the first important fact in the Agliati case. He affirmed with official certitude that only four passengers had left their seats during the flight: the country tradesman Giuseppe Sabelli was the first to visit the toilet before the banker; after his return, reporter Giorgio Vallesi had made a brief visit to the pilots in the cockpit; after that, the banker closeted himself in the toilet; after a further half an hour a second tradesman gave the alarm, having tried several times to open the locked door without success. The bigwig's two minions confirmed his statement, and the three of them were allowed to leave and catch another seaplane, arriving successfully in Palermo before dusk.

The Dornier Do-Wal 134 was, of course, grounded in its basin under strict police surveillance, awaiting a new and less perfunctory search. Boldrin began it under the influence of the bigwig's statement, but even though he was energetic and thorough, he failed to discover any new clues.

The hydroplane's layout was very simple. The cockpit was in the prow, with three places for the pilots and the mechanic. From there, a glass door opened into a vestibule, with the small toilet on the left and the exit door on the right. yond that, a second glass door led to the passenger cabin. When both doors were open, the passengers could see into the cockpit and the pilots could see the greater part of the passenger cabin, which was the plane's largest compartment, comprising two lines of six seats, each with a window. At the rear of the cabin was a wooden door which opened into the luggage compartment, which was triangular in shape and completely occupied the tail of the plane.

The fuselage itself only had a few openings: the exit door in the vestibule, which was kept locked during the flight and only opened after landing by the flight commander with a special key; a small skylight in the roof of the toilet; the twelve windows of the passenger cabin; and a large hatch in the roof of the luggage compartment, which could be opened from the outside or inside, and was used for loading and unloading luggage.

Boldrin searched slowly and very methodically in every corner, questioning the pilot and listening with great attention to his explanations, and checking the banker's seat. He examined the toilet, which was 1 metre square and 1 metre 70 in height. He barely looked at the floor and the walls, not believing for a single moment that their tin could hide any sort of deadly trap or secret passage, or any leak whatsoever, as Girini had declared in his own statement. Boldrin was far more interested in the small skylight. The flight commander had given him the precise measurements: 39 centimetres by 32. The small window, which was not locked, could be opened inwards by means of a handle, but was impossible to open outwards because of the tremendous air pressure, as Girini had duly explained.

The chief inspector took only a few brief notes. The plane had a very simple internal structure, and this very simplicity had a bad effect on his nerves. The search and the statements were pushing poor Boldrin down an investigative street which his instincts told him was a dead end.

Being a mere policeman, he wasn't particularly sensitive to a place's mood and atmosphere, but he began to find the tin walls of the small recess oppressive and suffocating, and he instinctively looked

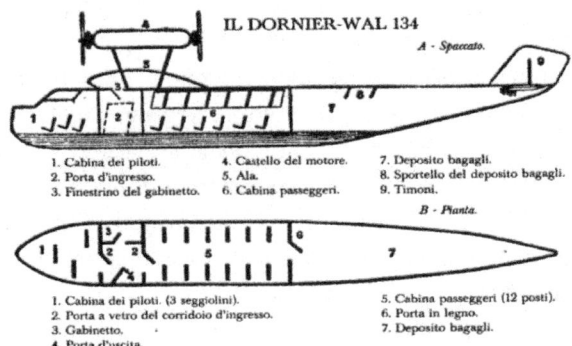

1. Cabina dei piloti.
2. Porta d'ingresso.
3. Finestrino del gabinetto.
4. Castello del motore.
5. Ala.
6. Cabina passeggeri.
7. Deposito bagagli.
8. Sportello del deposito bagagli.
9. Timoni.

1. Cabina dei piloti. (3 seggiolini).
2. Porta a vetro del corridoio d'ingresso.
3. Gabinetto.
4. Porta d'uscita.
5. Cabina passeggeri (12 posti).
6. Porta in legno.
7. Deposito bagagli.

A
1-cockpit
2-exit door
3-toilet window
4-motors
5-wings
6-passenger cabin
7-luggage compartment
8-luggage compartment door
9-helm

B
1-cockpit with three seats for the two pilots and the mechanic
2-glass door to cockpit
3-toilet
4-exit door
5 passenger cabin with 12 seats.
6-wooden door of luggage compartment.
7-luggage compartment

for a way out, in the hope that it was also Agliati's way out.

He looked again at the skylight. But unanimously the witnesses had described the banker as a tubby man with a paunch of considerable proportions, and it seemed quite impossible that he could have passed through the small window. It would have been an impossible operation even for poor Boldrin, with his own average width and height.

It could have been murder. It seemed the only possible solution, after having excluded an improbable deadly accident, and an even more improbable suicide. (Who would ever have decided to kill himself in a plane's toilet, without even knowing beforehand whether it was possible to throw himself from it?... And furthermore Boldrin had ascertained that it was absolutely impossible.)

But a murder demanded the malicious, deadly intervention of a third person at some point. Boldrin was too sensible to imagine a fantastic, murderous trap set by someone under poor Agliati's feet.

For a start, there was not a single clue to indicate the presence of a third person in the toilet, nor any indication that a trap had been placed, nor by whom. And how could any murderer foresee the banker's visit to the toilet at exactly the right moment? And what if another person had fallen into the trap? In any case, the bigwig's statement rendered an external intervention in the toilet quite impossible. It was ridiculous to think that someone could have already been hidden in that small space, and all the passengers were present and accounted for when the banker entered the toilet.

Only Sabelli, the country tradesman, had gone into the toilet before the banker, and he hadn't noticed anything suspicious. In any case, he was out of there many minutes before the banker's arrival. The reporter Giorgio Vallesi had gone past the door twice, once going to the cockpit and once returning to the cabin, but he hadn't had time to do anything at all. And the same could be said of Marchetti, the second tradesman. His repeated assaults on the locked door could have been vaguely suspicious, but he'd only been out of his seat for a few moments before he began.

In any case, even if Marchetti or someone else could theoretically have entered the small space, there were no traces whatsoever of breaking and entering on the small but solid lock, or on the small but very efficient inside bolt. And how was it possible to make the banker's body disappear into thin air?

Boldrin had only one possible explanation. The Foreign Office bigwig had only talked about his fellow passengers, and his statement confirmed only his and their movements. He couldn't have checked the actions of the crew members or, above all, those of the mysterious clandestine passenger who had absolutely had to fly on the Dornier Do-Wal 134.

He hoped very much that further questioning of passengers and crew would yield further clues in his investigation, and thus break the solid tin walls of the mysterious toilet. So he returned to his office in the airport, determined to spend all night, if necessary, interrogating each passenger and crew member separately.

The small, dark typist assigned to him by SANA airlines was already there in the office. She seemed very happy about the new job, which would not only satisfy her natural curiosity, but would also place her at the centre of a sensational mystery on everyone's lips, with the alluring prospect of being interviewed by many reporters. Her only misgiving was the tough policeman's reluctance to be forthcoming.

But the small, dark typist was mistaken. Poor Boldrin would have liked nothing more than to discuss the details of the case with someone, if only he could have explained his too few theories and his too many doubts. Desperate as he was to unearth promising leads from his interrogations, he confined himself to merely dictating the list of items found in the banker's briefcase, which had been left on his cabin seat.

In it, he had found a considerable quantity of papers and documents covered with numbers, and pencilled notes on the headed notepaper of the Italy & Greece Bank, where Agliati occupied the position of CEO.

Also amongst the papers, Boldrin had found a six-day first-class return railway ticket from Naples to Brindisi Marittima, valid until that very same day, July 12th. It seemed very likely that Agliati had arrived in Brindisi from Athens, where he lived, on July 6th. Apparently, he had only intended to go to Naples, and so hadn't bought a ticket to Rome. But something had necessitated him going to Rome and he had been obliged to remain there until that morning. Having apparently intended to stay for a couple of hours in Naples before his return, his only option had been to take the Ostia plane if he wanted to be back in Brindisi by dusk, as a quick check of the railway timetable confirmed: if he had wanted to be in Brindisi by the evening, he would have had to catch the five past three train from Naples. If Agliati had taken the quarter to nine train from Rome Termini, he could only have stayed in Naples for a short while, whereas the plane gave him the chance to remain in Rome a couple of hours longer. Certainly a car would have given him the same opportunity, but....

Boldrin shrugged off Agliati's predilection for planes and called Flight Commander Girini.

3- AN ASSISTANT COMMISSIONER, A CHIEF INSPECTOR AND THIRTEEN SUSPECTS

Assistant Commissioner Luigi Renzi scanned the morning newspapers rapidly. They were dedicating the most hysterical titles in their very rich repertoire to *THE FLYING BOAT MYSTERY*, but with the same sparse details of the evening before. The questioning of the witnesses was scarcely mentioned, but they did at least list the passengers' names, and Renzi immediately recognised one of them: his college friend Giorgio Vallesi.

Their friendship had begun when Giorgio entered the university and had been strengthened by four years of lazy wandering in the streets of Rome. It had survived the break after graduation and still remained warm and cordial, even if lacking the immediate, direct frankness of those earlier years.

THE FLYING BOAT MYSTERY, as it had been dubbed by *Il Messaggero*, had immediately attracted Luigi's attention and, when he discovered that his friend was mixed up in the tangle, he headed straight to Police Headquarters.

Renzi held a very unusual position in the Italian police force. He had signed up out of passion and curiosity, and a small inheritance permitted him a far more luxurious standing than the vast majority of his colleagues. On top of that, his great independence was afforded by the protection of his uncle, a highly-placed member of the Home Office's hierarchy who, although not enchanted by his nephew's choice of career, had felt himself obliged to look after a member of his own family. Renzi had accepted the situation grudgingly, in the hope that it would help him escape betrothal to the awful cousin his uncle had earmarked for him.

In any case, his uncle's protection was very helpful when he requested to be sent to Naples. His intervention in the Agliati case investigation was by no means harmful to the Naples police: after all, the Do-Wal 134 passengers came from Rome, they resided in Rome— or in any case in Latium—and a Roman policeman's help could be highly desirable.

So it was that Renzi rushed from Piazza Collegio Romano straight to the train station, and within three hours was partaking of a very quick breakfast in Naples before introducing himself to Chief Inspector Boldrin.

Good old Boldrin would have welcomed him warmly in any case, but, crushed by his responsibility, the intervention of another party was doubly welcome:

'As you can readily understand, Dr. Renzi'—in Italy as in Germany, the title of Doctor is bestowed upon any official or important person as a sign of respect, like knighthoods in England—'I've been able to detain passengers and crew members up till now, but I can't hold them forever. I don't have any proof, I don't have a single clue... and everybody is protesting fiercely! They want to be free again....'

'They're right, I'm afraid. It's only a teeny-weeny abuse of power on your part, my dear Boldrin.'

'Should I have let them go?' asked Boldrin nervously.

'No, no, of course not! You've done very well, I admire your skill in detaining them until now!'

'But I can't detain them forever and ever. After all, the search....'

He showed the assistant commissioner the promotional plan of the Dornier Do-Wal 134 and gave a detailed explanation of his own search of the plane:

'Comandante Girini notwithstanding, I feel quite certain it was neither accident nor suicide.'

'What's Girini's theory?'

'He strongly favours the suicide option.'

'Why not the accident?'

'Because of the position of the skylight. In order to have fallen from the plane, the banker would have to have climbed through it to get to the top of the fuselage.'

'That sounds like an absurd acrobatic exploit!'

'Furthermore, the dimensions of the skylight also rule out the suicide theory.'

'And if it's neither an accident nor a suicide, then it's inevitably murder, isn't? And the murderer, or at least an accomplice, must have been on board.'

'But we don't have a single reason for detaining them,' grumbled the poor chief inspector.

Renzi shrugged away his doubts:
'But you've already freed three of them.'
'You know, Dr. Renzi, they were—.'
'I know, I know, but were their statements at least useful?'
'They were of great value,' replied the chief inspector promptly. 'They are quite sure that only four passengers left their seats: a corn tradesman named Sabelli was in the toilet before the banker; a reporter named Vallesi visited the cockpit; the banker himself, of course, was in the toilet; and afterwards a fellow corn tradesman named Marchetti.'

Renzi listened absent-mindedly to the other's explanations, but he continued to study the plan, trying to perceive among its regular lines the still undistinguished shadows of the banker and his travel companions:

'Where were Sabelli and Marchetti seated?'
'At the back of the cabin, near the tail.'
'And Agliati?"
Boldrin reflected for a moment before answering:
'In the centre of the cabin, on the left.' He took the plan:
'Yes, fourth place on the left, there we are.'
Renzi followed his finger, mentally counting the seats:
'Twelve seats in six rows. All occupied, of course?'
'By thirteen passengers,' replied Boldrin, with a ghost of a smile.
'Thirteen?'
'The thirteenth passenger was a Metropolitan Bank teller named Larini. He arrived at the last moment, when the plane was full, and convinced the mechanic to give him his seat in the cockpit.'
'And the mechanic?'
'He travelled in the luggage compartment.'
Boldrin hesitated, noting the assistant commissioner's anxious astonishment:
'Of course, this hurried departure can be—.'
'And the flight commander?' Renzi cut him off.
'It was probably rash of him to accede to the insistent pleas of the passenger, and the mechanic—who certainly didn't want to lose his tip. And the plane was ready to take off... In any case, Larini didn't leave his place in the cockpit during the flight, as both pilots have confirmed in their separate statements.'

'And if he'd gone to the toilet, he would have been seen by the other passengers.'

'Yes, through the glass door.'

'And the mechanic?'

'He justified what he did by saying that nobody would have refused a few one hundred lire notes!'

'No, no, I was merely asking if during the flight....'

'He came out of the luggage compartment to go into the cockpit, but he returned almost immediately. The young reporter noticed that he had a parcel under his arm.'

The assistant commissioner looked him curiously.

'He claimed that it only contained the bread and fruit he usually ate during the flight, and the commander immediately confirmed that.'

Luigi Renzi remained silent, apparently accepting the simple explanation.

'We can go on to the passengers now.'

He read with a certain astonishment the list Boldrin had put together:

'The lady in red?'

The embarrassed Boldrin smiled wryly:

'Well, her true name is....'

After each passenger or crew member was questioned, Boldrin had allocated himself five minutes to summarising their statements. He never took notes during the interrogation for fear of disrupting the flow. Witnesses are always less spontaneous in their statements if they are worrying about any imprudent words being officially recorded.

His secretary rushed to answer his sudden ring.

'There are two ladies waiting in the lobby. Please send the older one in.'

The young typist had already begun to consider poor old Boldrin a bit of a cad. Now he was calling a fascinating woman not a day older than thirty-five "the older one." She answered with a small nod of indignation and went out to call the lady in question.

'Commissario, will you be letting me go? ' the lady implored.

Boldrin answered slowly in response to her anxious look:

'Of course, I would never permit myself to detain you.'

Her pleading was immediately replaced by indignation. Seeing her looking at him scornfully, he decided to use a brusquer tone:

'Your name is Vanna Sandrelli?'

Her short red felt brim lowered itself suddenly, whilst her twitching hands gripped the small, dainty handkerchief:

'Vanna Sandrelli, yes.'

She appeared oddly ashamed of her own name.

'Are you from Rome?'

''From Rome, yes.'

Apparently she was ashamed of her home town as well.

Boldrin made a brisk gesture with his hand:

'May I see your ticket, please?'

The lady in red hastened to open her bag whilst the stunned Chief Inspector Boldrin strived to conceal his own astonishment. Not being a fashion expert like Vallesi, he wasn't offended by its clashing lizard-green colour, but by the clashing monogram on the gilded catch: VF.

He looked absent-mindedly at the properly stamped OSTIA-PALERMO air ticket, then searched for an explanation of his doubts:

'Your maiden name, please?'

'My... Yes, Antonini.'

Boldrin tried to look solemn and officious:

'In that case, may I know where you found this bag, which does not, apparently, display the right initials?'

The lady in red looked at the policeman with confused anxiety, as if trying to work out the required right initials, then employed her residual energy for a shout of protest:

'No, no, no! '

Three negatives are far less solid and convincing than one, so Boldrin felt himself vindicated and leant towards her with an insinuating look:

'And you won't tell me why you went to Palermo either?'

The red felt brim was flapping nervously from left to right, so Boldrin got up from his chair with an ominous look:

'Signora, I don't need to remind you that it's in your best interests to tell the truth and only the truth, as dutifully requested. I think that a moment of quiet reflection should convince you of this very simple fact, but rest assured that we shall find the truth in any case. Until that moment, you will be detained at our disposal.'

The woman in red tried to protest. Boldrin hoped that her rebellious look would translate into very revealing words, but the only result was a violent slamming of the door as she left.

Renzi's response to that little tale was a vague shake of the head, before proceeding to read another name loudly from the list:
'Marcella Arteni.'
'Ah, that girl! I begin to ask the usual questions, where are you from, where are you going and why, and she replies that she's going to Palermo for "family reasons." When I insist, she tells me that she's aware that it's my duty to question her and that she will promptly and dutifully give me the required answers, but she has not the slightest intention of telling me more about her travel to Palermo.'

Renzi smiled to himself, imagining the solid frame of the policeman pinned back in his chair by an outburst of energetic feminine grace.

Boldrin was not blessed with methods and logic of a great detective. A world-famous sleuth, with his nose pressed against that high and impenetrable feminine wall, would have built a stairway of theories and hypotheses for climbing over it to achieve his ends. Plain, simple Boldrin had instead plainly and simply accepted the situation with his own natural good sense, not throwing himself into a sea of imaginative explanations where his total lack of clues and information would have ended up drowning him. So Renzi asked no more and returned once again to the passenger list:

'Augusto and Maria Martelli.'
'By contrast, those two talked too much... Ah, how they talked! Signora Martelli, in particular. A lengthy rigmarole about a dying uncle in Palermo, a promised inheritance and the malice of a scheming maid, and so on, and so on. If you want to interrogate them again, I think that you will be far more able to orient yourself.'
'Of course, of course, I will hear the Martellis' rigmarole with pleasure. And now, Giorgio Vallesi....'
'Ah, the young reporter! Brisk, intelligent, and with too much fantasy for my humble taste.'

Renzi smiled knowingly.
'For Vallesi, everybody was nervous and very suspicious: Agliati was worried and anxious; the lady in red was a bag of nerves; the mechanic was fishy; the clandestine passenger was certainly crooked and the two pilots....'

'Good old Giorgio! He's always the same! I remember when we were at university together... yes, yes, I've known him for ages! And I will be very happy to interview the reporter myself!'

Boldrin answered with a smile, but his eyes and mind were attracted by the next name....

The third corn tradesman, Bertieri, had entered the dark office with a fierce scowl on his swarthy face, and his violent words had immediately shattered the quiet calm.

Bertieri protested with all his strength about the police brutally detaining him without questioning—him a peaceful citizen. Boldrin was startled by these fierce protests, but a calm and authoritative look at peaceful citizen Bertieri rendered him more and more peaceful, reducing his flaming outburst to nothing more than a very soft whisper.

'So, you are calling yourself Bertieri today? Have you abandoned the emigration racket, or do you make them travel by plane these days?'

Bertieri had been calling himself Pagelli when Boldrin had arrested him, some years ago, for an unsavoury business of Italian emigrants to the United States. Now, he tried to respond with dignity to the policeman's smug irony:

'That's all in the past, Commissario. Now we are living in the present! I'm straight now, I earn my living honestly.'

'And pigs can fly with you on the plane! What a luxurious life you lead, Pagelli. Did you get a big inheritance from a Dutch uncle in the States?'

'I repeat, I'm straight. I'm an honest and peaceful citizen, and the bank pays my air fare.'

'A bank? What kind of a bank, if you please?'

Bertieri answered after a moment's hesitation:

'The Italy and Argentina Bank sent me to Tunis to deal with a newspaper.'

'Do you take me for a fool? Please invent a better fairy-tale.'

'It's the truth, the whole truth and nothing but the plain and simple truth, Commissario. Look at my passport.'

Boldrin examined it very carefully, and the visa for Tunisia was indeed as regular as clear water. Bertieri showed him a letter as well, addressed to A J Morangis, Directeur du "Simoun", 2 Rue de Naples, Tunis.

'As you can see, I'm straight,' repeated the alleged corn tradesman.

'Straight as a crooked arrow, Pagelli. Your flight to Tunis doesn't convince me even for a second. Why didn't you fly directly from Ostia to Tunis? It would have been a swifter and more luxurious trip,' smiled the policeman, without shaking the brazen and slightly ironic tradesman one little bit.

'You are not so well-informed, Commissario. The plane to Tunis is only on Mondays, Wednesdays and Fridays. Today is Tuesday, so....'

Boldrin hid his irritation by changing the subject of the questioning suddenly:

'And are your travel companions also as straight as you? Where do they send the emigrants? To Argentina?'

'I don't think so, but honestly I only met them on the Terminal bus, so I can't swear to their own morality, I'm afraid.'

Renzi interrupted Boldrin's tale about Bertieri:
'What can you tell me about the other two, Sabelli and Marchetti?'

'Not so much, and not so convincingly. They are corn tradesman travelling to Sicily for a big trade contract, apparently.'

'And they were travelling by plane?'

'They told me they didn't want to lose any time and that they loved to experience the emotion of flight,' replied Boldrin with angry scepticism. 'And there's something else about them; look at this suitcase, please.'

He opened a big and almost new fibre suitcase. On the rough canvas lining, under the Franzi label, he indicated, close to the hinges, a series of numbers written with a violet pencil.

8615915252241285   1519

Boldrin picked up a half-empty glass bottle:
'I wouldn't even have noticed them if the Eau de Cologne had not been spilt on the lining, rendering the numbers far more visible.'

Renzi repeated each single number loudly, then repeated them in an irregular, broken rhythm, trying to find a pattern in the sound.

'What do you think about that, Dr.Renzi? I admit that this series of numbers has intrigued me from the beginning, maybe far too much. It could just be a totally unimportant annotation made by the tradesmen.'

'Of course,' replied Renzi, in a non-committal tone, which would allow him to formulate any sort of fantastic hypothesis.

'Certainly, we can't be sure that these numbers had anything to do with our case. But if they were indeed a code or a cipher....'

He had a moment of hesitation, but the assistant commissioner's silence pushed him to continue:

'Perhaps the last numbers, 1519, separate from the others, could be a sort... I don't know... a sort of signature?'

'Why not?' said the assistant commissioner in a kindly manner. 'But couldn't they just be, instead of a cipher, a simple series of numbers, annotated casually on the first surface to hand, as you do, for instance, when you are on the telephone? Let me try a little experiment... I'm very perplexed about the last numbers, I admit, so I'll try to ignore them for the moment. That leaves sixteen numbers, and we can divide them into three almost similar groups: 861591, 52522, and 41285... Couldn't they be simply three telephone numbers?'

'Telephone numbers? But from where? From which town?'

'Possibly Rome, but I'm not sure.'

Boldrin was actually quite convinced by this explanation, but he tried all the same to express a certain scepticism:

'Excuse me, Dr. Renzi, but why are you making a first group of six numbers, when the other two have only five in them? Why don't you try other possible combinations, like 86159, 152522, 41285, or 86159, 15252, 241285, or....'

'Yes, yes, of course anything is possible, but telephone numbers beginning with 1 or 2 don't exist in Rome or in any other town, as far as I know....For instance 861591 could itself refer to the new Quartiere Nomentano standard, and even the five numbers groups could be Rome telephone numbers... Would you allow me to try the Phone Information Service?'

He dialled the number and spoke to the switchboard operator:

'I'd like to check three telephone numbers for a police investigation, please. I'm Vice Questore Luigi Renzi from Rome Police Headquarters. Good, the three numbers are... Thanks a lot, Signorina,

35

you've been very helpful... Good news, Boldrin, we've found the numbers of a lawyer named Cassese, of a good carpenter named Sannizzola, and, last but not least, of Cavalier Sandri, assistant managing director of the Italy & Argentina Bank.'

'Pagelli's bank! Ostrega! Holy Bread!'

'Indeed.' Renzi smiled quietly.

'So, there is a connection with the banker's disappearance?'

'Possibly.' Renzi was far more calm and thoughtful than the easily excitable chief inspector. 'But we can't say for sure before re-interrogating Sabelli and Marchetti.'

'I will recall them immediately!'

'Wait a minute, if you please.' Renzi always preferred to take stock and weigh the effect of each new clue in an imaginary ledger before proceeding. 'Before any more questioning, it is helpful to summarise any suspicions we may have about each of the individuals on board.'

The chief inspector's sigh merely expressed his total distrust of any form of logical deduction:

'If that's what you want.'

Renzi tried to be persuasive:

'That way we can decide who will be questioned again by me. Please correct me if I don't have all the facts crystal clear in my mind... Apart from the three witnesses you released, we have twelve people on board. Comandante Girini is of excellent character and never left his place before the banker's disappearance became known. Secondo Pilota Vandelli has an excellent record as well and he, too, never left his place before landing. The mechanic Franceschi was in the luggage compartment and left it once very briefly, after the banker was locked in the toilet, and a second time when the passengers gave the alarm. Signora Sandrelli or Antonini—.'

'Both names are false! The Rome Police don't know anything about a Signora Sandrelli or Antonini....'

'Of course, but remember also that she never left her seat! Signorina Arteni—.'

'I asked for information about her, too!'

'Good, so we can decide if we wish to question her again... Vallesi never left his seat... excuse me, he left it to pay a brief visit to the cockpit before the banker's own deadly visit to the toilet! The Martellis... Yes, yes, I will hear their rigmarole for myself. I adore stories about dying uncles and scheming maidservants!... Bertieri, or Pagelli....'

'A very fishy and slippery customer, this one.' Boldrin seemed quite affectionate towards his old foe. 'I bet—.'

'Don't bet anything, please. He never left his seat!'

'In any case, I asked for information about him from the Italy & Argentina Bank. I'm not at all persuaded by his trip to Tunis, and I would love to see that Tunisian reporter's face!'

Renzi had a mysterious smile on his lips:

'Oh, there'll be a Tunisian reporter's face, you can be sure! And so we arrive at Sabelli and Marchetti, two supposed corn tradesmen taking a plane trip for not very convincing reasons. Sabelli visited the toilet before Agliati. Afterwards, Marchetti tried to open the locked door several times, but would he have attracted so much attention to himself if he'd really been involved in Agliati's disappearance? And in any case, he only left his seat for a few moments....'

'You seem to be forgetting the famous phone numbers in his suitcase,' said Boldrin zealously.

'I eagerly await his explanations about them.' Once more Renzi dismissed the good chief inspector's suggestion with a pinch of concealed irony. 'So that only leaves us with the mysterious bank teller Larini, who was able to leave Rome on a full plane, thanks to the mechanic's kind intervention. How did he justify his urgent departure?'

'He'd been asked to carry some urgent documents to the Palermo branch of Metropolitan Bank. They were very important and secret papers, and had to be carried by a confidential courier.'

'We shall check his story, of course,' said Renzi slowly, as if he were trying to grasp some unforeseen meaning in the words Boldrin had just uttered. 'But the good bank teller, too, remained in his seat, in full view of the pilots.' There was another moment of hesitation, then he continued:

'Is there anything else, Commissario?'

'No, I'm afraid not,' sighed Boldrin.

Renzi added in a more lively tone:

'We must remember also to check out the banker. After all, he's our leading actor, isn't he? He was an Italian citizen, wasn't he?'

'He's Italian by birth, but when he established himself in Athens some years ago he took Greek citizenship.'

'We shall ask about him in Greece, then.'

Boldrin sighed once again. Apparently he was not all that interested in Agliati's past history:

'Of course, and in the meantime you'll question the Martellis, Sabelli and Marchetti, Vanna Sandrelli—.'

'And Signorina Arteni, of course. But I think I can spare our lady in red further questioning.'

'Wouldn't it be better....'

'If you please... but could you repeat her two names again?'

'She called herself Signora Sandrelli.'

'And her maiden name was Antonini? Good....so we agree about the new questionings, do we not? Sorry, now I'm going to interview the reporter!'

So saying, he left the office; only when the echo of his footsteps had faded did the sighing chief inspector find the strength to raise himself from his throne.

4-TWO FRIENDS

Renzi looked through the first door to his right.

Seated at a table in the middle of the room, the tall, blond and lean Flight Commander Girini was speaking in a brief staccato to his second-in-command, an utterly insignificant little man who limited himself to nodding his approval. The man seated some distance away from them with the dark, calm face and traces of grease and oil on his hands was obviously Franceschi, the mechanic.

Renzi closed the door softly. A hubbub of voices drew his attention towards the part of the room where the passengers were gathered. Pagelli-Bertieri, the two other tradesmen, and the fortyish middle-class couple were seated near the door. Larini, the teller, was sitting by himself, looking very isolated. Signorina Arteni and the woman in red were seated near the window, with Vallesi standing next to the girl, leaning against the glass pane. He was looking at her so intently that he only noticed Renzi after the latter had called out to him:

'Hi, Giorgio!'

'Oh, Luigi! Are you here to——.'

'Yes,' Renzi interrupted him hastily. '*La Tribuna* dispatched me as soon as they heard the news.'

'Ah, *La Tribuna*... good!'

Vallesi was too astonished to say anything, but Renzi was doing the talking for the two of them:

'Ah, you lucky fellow! You were on the spot! Could you introduce me to your lady friends?'

Giorgio spoke immediately to Marcella:

'Signorina Arteni, may I introduce you to my great friend Luigi Renzi?'

He realised grudgingly that he was overlooking the lady in red and so he repeated the introduction, mumbling her name unintelligibly.

'I imagine that you were trying desperately to not speak about the mystery?' observed Luigi jokingly.

'Quite so,' replied Marcella gaily, giving him a beautiful smile.

'I confess that in your company, Signorina Arteni, it would be wiser to find far pleasanter arguments of conversation...but your wonderful eyes could be equally suited to read a mystery novel or my newspaper tomorrow!'

The lady in red's hazel eyes watched the gallant Renzi, scandalized, whilst Marcella accepted the compliment and mumbled simply:

'My wonderful eyes... Thank you very much.'

Vallesi muttered something, trying to hide his discomfort, but Luigi was too pleased with his own little comedy:

'Please, Giorgio, I'm working!'

Suddenly the lady in red seemed to rouse herself:

'Are you a reporter? The newspapers will print the names of the persons....'

'All the names that we shall discover in any possible and impossible way, Signora. I confess that I asked Giorgio to introduce me to both of you....' He smiled at the two ladies. 'Also to learn your names. But now I must rush to use my very useful information!'

He pushed his friend out of the room, finally facing the latter's protests:

'May I know the meaning of this farce? Why did you want to be introduced to—.'

Renzi smiled ironically, pleased:

'To your new conquest? Don't you find it quite natural that I would want to know the passengers of that mysterious flying boat better? Particularly because they seem to be very interesting... in every possible way.' He smiled again.

Giorgio seemed almost as scandalized as the lady in red.

'Don't you understand when I'm joking any more? But I'm totally serious when I tell you that Signorina Arteni is very beautiful,' Renzi added, as a wicked sting in the tail. 'Ah, if I could be really a *Tribuna* reporter, and not the Roman police official sleuth! The poor detective wanting to know really what happened has nothing in hand, whereas the lucky reporter has everything he needs: a mysterious disappearance, a very modern and novel setting, two beautiful ladies....'

'The woman in red,' mumbled a perplexed Giorgio.

'Sorry, but you could at least be clearer when you pronounce her name!'

'How can I be clearer if I'm pronouncing a name I don't know?'

'Pity, I'd hoped you'd be better than poor old Boldrin, pushing a beautiful lady to confide her secrets to you.'

Vallesi gaped at the new, but perhaps not too stunning, horizons of suspicion opened by the news:

'She refused to give her name to the police?'

'Worse: she gave two names and both of them are false!'

'I told the chief inspector that she seemed very nervous. She was apparently eager to get to Palermo, and never took her eyes off Agliati!'

Giorgio was now very enthusiastically on the lady in red's trail. Apparently he was pleased with himself for having noticed something about her. "Something"! Luigi had forever wanted to cancel that irritating, utterly depressing, silly word! Someone once said that the Italian dictionary is made of only two words: "thing" and "stuff". Against the lady in red he had "something" and nothing more. And he also had "something" against Signorina Arteni, the girl in blue... Something, always only something!

'Boldrin had told you that Pagelli was very suspicious about the beautiful girl's agitation when Agliati's long absence was noticed by the passengers. She was astonished that it was a banker that had disappeared, apparently....'

Luigi pointed wickedly at his friend:

'Signorina Arteni, too, was suspicious? Did you notice "something" about her?'

'I don't know anything at all about her. I only met her on board!'

Luigi smiled, noting Giorgio's habitual infatuation with some girl... He would never change! He was on the verge of telling him that she had refused to inform the police about her reason for travelling to Palermo, but he was happy to remain silent when Vallesi himself hastened to change the subject, returning again to the lady in red:

'I tell you, Luigi, the lady in red was very agitated about the banker....'

'And the banker himself was very nervy and agitated as well, wasn't he?'

'Oh, I wouldn't say that; he was simply not too pleased to be constantly observed by her... And she gave a false name to the police?'

'She called herself Signora Sandrelli, but Boldrin noticed the initials on the bag were VF! And her maiden name apparently was Antonini, so....'

Vallesi was very thoughtful:

'I noticed her bag, too, as you can well imagine. A green bag with a red dress!'

'I can readily understand your horror.' Luigi smiled at his friend. 'But I don't think that the disgustingly clashing bag was stolen. And I'm not that interested in the mystery of the bag. Quite possibly it has no connection at all with the banker's disappearance. And in any case I've just solved it, and am only waiting for a phone confirmation about it....'

Hearing a phone ringing, Luigi went back into the office and re-emerged in the corridor, looking very pleased with himself.

'I can confirm to you that the lady in red is called Vanna Ferrari; that she's married to an engineer named Adolfo Ferrari, and she lives in via del Tritone....'

'So the VF bag really is hers!'

Luigi eyed his friend. He seemed strangely astonished, possibly because he'd hoped for far more sensational news.

'But how did you find her real name?'

Renzi smiled knowingly at his friend again, ready to play the master detective:

'It's very simple: she gave the police two wrong names, Sandrelli and Antonini, which counts against her, and neither name corresponded to the initials on the bag. During the flight she seemed very nervy and agitated, and she was very hysterical during Boldrin's questioning. Her answers were extremely ambiguous and completely contradictory. Which means she can't be your typical hardened criminal.'

'So, an anxious and very excitable lady is being questioned by a policeman. She wants to hide her name, so she has to find another one. When she's asked about her maiden name, she suddenly needs to find a second invention, but she's not used to lying and her imagination is not at all fertile or swift, so she quite understandably falls back on a name familiar to her. It seemed very likely that the maiden name she gave was actually the right one. She was on her way from Rome to Palermo, and if there wasn't a Signora Sandrelli or a Signorina Antonini in Rome, as Boldrin had verified, maybe there was one in Palermo. So I asked the Palermo police about a Signor or

Signora Sandrelli or Antonini, having a married daughter living in Rome, and they found a widow named Antonini with a daughter named Vanna, living in Rome and married to an engineer named Ferrari.'

Renzi was clearly very pleased with himself.

Giorgio remained silent, trying to grasp the consequences of the discovery:

'Well, my congratulations, but we don't know yet why she's flying to Palermo and why she acted in such a nervous and mysterious way. Why was she so anxious? Why did she lie to the police? Why did she hide her real married name?'

Vallesi was trying to push his friend along that path, and he was also trying to convince himself that it was the right one.

'I hope you won't assume she's innocent, just because you succeeded in identifying her!'

'Certainly not, but we do know something more about her, in any case.'

But Renzi wasn't thinking about the lady in red but about Signorina Arteni, and her actions once she was freed. So he was very happy to see her again in the chief inspector's office.

She was with an older man, who was angrily confronting poor old Boldrin, and who was clearly her father. He was not particularly tall, but he was well-built, with rich, smooth grey hair. He looked at Renzi with pale grey eyes under thick, dark brows. At fifty or so, he was still a very good-looking man. Boldrin introduced the assistant commissioner:

'Dr.Renzi, may I present Signorina Arteni and her father, Commendatore Arteni?'

Arteni made a frosty bow, and Marcella's impudent eyes twinkled beneath the rim of her hat:

'I've just had the honour of being introduced to a very famous *Tribuna* reporter. What a lucky day for me!'

Boldrin was astonished by her remark, and Luigi smiled at the amusing and charming girl. But her father was looking angrily at his watch:

'So, before we go, I'm very happy to thank you, Commissario, for your kind understanding. We are returning to Rome, now, but rest assured that if we can help your investigations in any way....' He bowed again frostily to Renzi and made a triumphant exit with his daughter on his arm. Certainly, the man had no love for the police, and in particular Luigi Renzi.

'Sorry, Dr.Renzi,' mumbled poor old Boldrin. 'Commendatore Arteni took a train from Florence immediately, once he found out that his daughter had been detained in Naples. He met her in the lobby and asked to be introduced immediately.'

Renzi bit back a list of not-too-friendly questions and instead asked:

'Did he know the purpose of his daughter's trip?'

'He seemed quite informed about it, but he only spoke vaguely about very private family reasons, and clearly didn't want to be more precise in his explanations. But we had nothing against her, she couldn't possibly... and we'd already decided to release her anyway.'

Renzi cut through his excuses rudely:

'Did you know that I'd identified the lady in red?'

He was very satisfied by poor old Boldrin's amazement. After his explanation, he continued:

'And now we can re-interrogate the Martellis, Sabelli and Marchetti.'

Boldrin asked for Signora Martelli, and we shall not describe her here, leaving it to the reader to imagine a middle-aged woman who hadn't even been beautiful at twenty, and who was embittered morally and physically by a gloomy, grey life enlivened only by small neighbourhood quarrels, alongside a dwarfish, feeble husband whom she dominated completely, even as she was unable to push him up the social staircase to a head clerk's position. Boldrin asked her to explain the reason for her trip to Palermo and a torrent of words gushed out:

'Ah, Commissario, you know, there is our uncle, my Augusto's poor mother's stepbrother, who's now more on the other side than on this one, if you see what I mean. He's no longer a spring chicken, his age is a big burden for everyone, and with a double pneumonia, you know... Of course we knew that he was ill, but not how ill, and it's a long way to Palermo, Commissario, you can't go to Palermo every day, can you? But early this morning we got a cable informing us about his very serious state of health. He's practically dead and buried, it's only a matter of days if not hours.'

'So you took the plane?'

'When you must, you must. It wasn't the time to be miserly and meagre, Commissario. Strictly between us, Commissario, this uncle of ours has some savings, not so much, you know, we are all poor as church mice in the family, only cobwebs and flies in our pockets, but he promised to leave everything to my Augusto. He's not a real uncle, but, you know, Commissario, there's not so much of a family around, and my Augusto is the only leftover, as you might say... But you know, Commissario, he had that hag of a maidservant for ages, and we were afraid of some dirty trick on her part. Never trust servants, Commissario, they're always ready to jump on the loot in the end. So, when a friend of ours cabled the sad news from Palermo, I immediately said to my Augusto: "Dearest, that uncle of yours will not live another day, the poor thing. Upon my soul, he has both feet in the grave, so don't be mean as usual, open your wallet and let's take the plane! Please, make an effort, we can't arrive just for the burial, fresh and jolly as nightingales, we simply must arrive beforehand, and when you must, you must."'

The torrent suddenly dried up, and the subsequent answers failed to provide any explanations to poor Boldrin. The flow started again when he tried desperately to free himself of her overbearing presence. Maria Martelli was apparently trying not to irritate the policeman and she fought to contain her normal acrid and domineering voice:

'As you can see, Commissario, we are good, honest and obedient citizens, very respectful of your authority. We've waited and waited and waited until now, even though this awful delay is a disaster for us, as you can readily understand. We took the plane, with a great sacrifice of our meagre savings, and now we are here in Naples when our wretched uncle is dying in Palermo, the poor thing, the wretched hag is plotting, the wretched clock is ticking...Now you've questioned us twice, so, Commissario, may we finally leave? We've lost a full day, Commissario, a full day, and planes aren't as cheap as bread, you know.'

Boldrin tried to reassert his authority. He raised himself from his chair with an official look on his face:

'Signora Martelli, justice must always follow its course, its rules and procedures, always and in every case. You and your husband will be free to leave when, and only when, the circumstances allow it.'

But, once she was out of the room, he looked anxiously at his

supervisor, who nodded his approval immediately:
'Well done, I leave you the husband. He's yours!'
Boldrin immediately faced the new witness:
'Are you going to Palermo, Signor Martelli?'
Martelli's pale eyes wandered around the room, as if he was searching for his dear wife.
'Why did you take a plane?'
'Well, I have un uncle, my poor mother's stepbrother... He lives in Palermo... Well, he lived because he's dying... They cabled us... He's very seriously ill, the poor man, a double—yes, a double—pneumonia... but the passing years are always a burden for everyone, aren't they?'

Luigi rolled his eyes, the words were buzzing in his ears, as if he'd heard them before...

Augusto Martelli was continuing very slowly, as if he was weighing every single word cautiously:

'You know, the poor man had some savings, not so much, and he promised to leave them to me... we have no other relatives, you know, but there is a hag of a maid...he had her for ages and we fear some dirty trick from her... So, when the cable arrived, my wife—.'

The assistant commissioner's sudden outburst stopped the methodical drip, drip of words:

'If you want to give your fantasy a little rest Signor Martelli....'

The other fluttered his pale eyes, even as his lips kept moving under the pressure of the coaching he'd received. Luigi continued with kind irony:

'So you can be a bit more varied in your inventions.'

He had suddenly understood why Martelli's words were buzzing insistently in his ears with a curious sensation of déjà vu: he had heard them, equal and identical, only ten minutes before from his wife, word for word, comma for comma... So Martelli was only repeating what his dear wife had coached him to do.

'I don't understand.'

'That's not important. It's far better to tell the truth in these cases, you know.'

'Really, my poor uncle... ' Martelli stuck to his story as desperately as a gluttonous boy clutching a piece of cake.

Boldrin exploded with official violence:

'Leave your uncle aside. We knew immediately it was all a story concocted by your wife. Do you understand what it means to lie to the police?'

The only effect of the melodramatic outburst was to seal poor Martelli's lips tightly; although he was, quite naturally, afraid of the police, he was even more terrified of his overbearing wife. So all they could do was to send the heroic husband away, at which Luigi commented that it would have been far more effective to attack Signora Martelli:

'The only foundation in his wretched life is the terror inspired by his abominable wife. All we can do is to try to convince his boss that it's futile to persist with their ridiculous story. Possibly, her husband will inspire an ounce of his holy terror in her! And now, we shall tackle Marchetti and Sabelli.'

Boldrin was unhappy about his recent outburst, so he was quite happy to leave the job of questioning to his superior.

Luigi asked Marchetti:

'You're going to Palermo with your friend, Signor Sabelli, aren't you? And you're signing a corn deal, I believe. Who arranged it?'

'Sabelli.'

'Why you, and not someone else?'

'We're friends, for goodness sake, and—well, Sabelli knows that corn is my field, my area of expertise.'

'And what is Sabelli's area of expertise?'

Marchetti's only answer was a ghost of a smile, but Luigi continued, as if he hadn't noticed it:

'You weren't surprised to hear a corn deal proposal coming from him?'

This time Marchetti answered with a shrug, so Renzi changed the subject swiftly:

'Do you know Francesco Agliati?'

'Of course not!'

'And his bank, the Italy & Argentina Bank?'

Boldrin suppressed his surprise, but Marchetti answered quietly and firmly:

'Never.'

'But we found the managing director's phone number in your suitcase.'

'In my suitcase?'

'In your suitcase!'

Renzi could read only a frank and total astonishment in his eyes.

Boldrin pushed the suitcase towards him and Marchetti responded immediately:

'That's not mine, it's Sabelli's! There's been a mix-up with the labels, very possibly.'

'So you don't know anything about these numbers?' asked Boldrin.

Marchetti shrugged his complete ignorance again.

'You were both in a hotel in Rome this week, I believe?' asked Renzi.

'Yes, at the Continental, in adjoining rooms.'

'And you both had telephones, didn't you? Were there no calls, yesterday?'

'Not for me.'

'And for Sabelli?'

'I don't know, I was out of my room for much of the time.'

'And now for the mysterious Signor Sabelli....'

Once Giuseppe Sabelli was in the office, Luigi asked him:

'It's a very good time for corn, isn't it?'

Sabelli answered with a broad smile:

'Never been better!'

'Had you ever met Francesco Agliati before? Or have you dealt in the past with his bank, the Italy & Greece Bank? Oh, I'm sorry, it's the Italy & Argentina Bank, isn't it? They're closely connected, and it's easy to confuse them, you know.'

'Never heard of either of them.'

'So why is the managing director of the Italy & Argentina Bank's number marked on your suitcase?'

'On my... suitcase?'

Sabelli repeated the words several times, as if trying to grasp their meaning. His eyes briefly held a glint of terror and astonishment. But he recovered almost immediately and his eyes returned to being impenetrable bulwarks:

'I'm really stunned by the news. May I look at the suitcase myself?'

Renzi pushed it towards the hesitant Sabelli:

'I don't understand. Couldn't it be an annotation made in the factory, or in the shop?'

Luigi turned suddenly to face the window:

'Possibly.'

Sabelli understood his exit cue and swiftly left the office.

Boldrin gave his supervisor a friendly smile:

'What do you think about him?'

'Only that the corn market has been very low in the last two weeks.'

Boldrin hesitated, waiting for a confirmation of his words:

'Marchetti seemed sincere....'

'Possibly,' replied Renzi mechanically.

The good chief inspector was quite irritated by Renzi's evasive attitude. He seemed absent-minded, almost disinterested.

'So what we are doing with all these people?'

'Dear old Boldrin....'

Renzi's vague words seemed to suggest many things, and nothing at all, so the chief inspector sought to intervene with his solid common sense:

'We'll have to release all of them. We have nothing against anyone, do we?'

'Quite so,' the assistant commissioner smiled ruefully. 'Things are not going well for us. We can choose between an impossible accident, an impossible suicide, and an even more impossible murder.'

'And the murderer must have been on board,' added the chief inspector bitterly. 'But we haven't a single clue and we can't detain anybody. It would be quite dangerous to arrest someone without....'

'Absolutely. We must release all of them... keeping them under strict surveillance, of course.'

'I'll keep an eye on my fake Bertieri, don't you worry!'

'But please don't forget Sabelli and Marchetti, either!'

'And Larini the teller!'

Renzi and Boldrin were each listing their own favourites, like two bookmakers before a race.

'As for the others... I don't think it could be the case for Signorina Arteni, or your friend, the reporter,' insinuated Boldrin.

Renzi bowed ironically.

'Also, the lady in red seems now....'

'Now you're listing the white and black sheep,' smiled the assistant commissioner. 'But you must be careful: in every good mystery novel the culprit is the least likely suspect!'

Boldrin looked askance at the merry glint in his superior's eyes. He had never read a mystery novel; he was too busy with his own mysteries, thank you very much!

Now the man was serious again, as he checked railway timetables:

'Every passenger on the plane was flying to Palermo, I believe? Good. So we can release everybody now, including the crew; they'll be grounded for several days by SANA, and the Rome police can keep an eye on them. As for the passengers... it's half-past two now, and the first train to Palermo leaves at half-past six. However, ten minutes before that, there's a train leaving for Rome, and if someone decides to interrupt his travel... can I have a couple of detectives on hand?'

'Actually, I'm afraid I only have a couple,' replied Boldrin. 'Tonight there's a stake-out of a big gambling den, where we're hoping to surprise some very unsavoury characters.'

'Don't worry, two detectives are all I need for surveillance of the two trains.'

'You don't need them to fly to Palermo?'

'No, I don't think so. They would have to pass the night in Naples and arrive the following day at dusk, whereas the night train will be in Palermo by noon. I'll go to the station at six o'clock, so as to look every one of them in the eye before they board that night train. Only then will I decide whether I return to Rome or go to Palermo with them. Meanwhile, you can brief the Palermo and Rome police, so they will be able to help your detectives, and our friends will be kept under strict surveillance from the very moment of their arrival.'

'I'll take care of it, don't worry. Since they're all leaving Naples, my work here is ended, and I can only wish you....'

'And I can only thank you for your great and very kind help. In any case, I will keep you informed, and possibly we shall meet again in Rome....'

And they parted like two very old and very good friends.

5-THE TRIP TO PALERMO

6.23, 6.24, 6.25... the watch hands were making their patient and methodical daily trip. Giorgio and Luigi walked onto the platform, watching the passengers' movements whilst exchanging the occasional vague observation. The night express to Sicily was ready to leave. The Flying Boat Mystery had not turned out as promised for Giorgio, and he had announced his intention to return to Rome, whereas Luigi had decided to follow the other passengers to Palermo.

So, here the two of them were, awaiting the arrival of the others. The first to appear had been Signora Ferrari. She had arrived at the station half an hour too early, and Giorgio had commented:

'Anxious and agitated as usual, our lady in red! She seems always to leave every place in a hurry.'

The next to arrive had been Larini, gripping his official briefcase with his usual energy. Renzi had examined the many documents it contained with care. The most important ones concerned the possibility of a big joint venture involving the Palermo branch of Metropolitan Bank and the Corleone Regional Bank. The bank teller had chosen a second-class compartment, and he had been joined after a few minutes by the Martellis.

After a momentary embarrassment, the formidable Signora Martelli had marked her total disgust for the recurring travel companion and had hastened to choose a different compartment, followed immediately behind by her faithful husband.

6.25, 6.26... Here came Pagelli, the ex-convict, Boldrin's great favourite. Luigi asked himself if he was really going to Tunis and instinctively moved towards the train.

'So, are you really going to Palermo?' asked Vallesi. 'I'm only sorry not to have discovered anything about the two corn tradesmen. They're the only two missing passengers, and possibly I might have discovered something about them in Rome.'

'Marcella is missing, too!'

'I thought you would have remembered her. But her name hasn't been mentioned in vain, it appears. Look over there!'

Marcella's blue dress fluttered whilst she nimbly passed amongst the crowd.

'You're very lucky, she's still alone,' joked Luigi. 'And she's going to Palermo, instead of returning to Rome with her dear father!'

6.29, 6.30... Vallesi jumped when a booming voice announced the train's departure:

'All aboard!'

'Shall we go?' he asked Renzi.

The plural noun made Luigi smile, but he didn't say anything.

Slowly, the windows of the train passed before the eyes of the friends and relatives gathered on the platform for the last salutations.

'Torre Annunziata, Nocera, Cava dei Tirreni... Six-minute stop in Salerno....'

'Shall we walk a bit?' asked Vallesi.

'So that you can admire this beautiful train, now that you have decided to follow me to Palermo?'

Vallesi appeared slightly hurt by his friend's teasing.

Luigi wondered if his friend was really considering a serious relationship with Marcella. Certainly she had plenty of admirers, but Giorgio, too had talked about many girls. Remembering the girl in blue's slender figure, he gave a little sigh as he thought about his friend's luck. If only... Yes, if only... But he raised his chin resolutely. After all, the girl had abandoned her father once again, in order to hurry off mysteriously to Palermo... Why?

He walked silently with his friend along the grey platform of Salerno station. Even in that gorgeous summer evening, the twilight was sneakily insinuating a sad vein of dreary loneliness. Giorgio's motive became clear when they saw the restaurant-car's small red lamps on the homely and inviting white table-cloths, with the ever-alluring possibility of a chance meeting with the beautiful Marcella....

The train started once again on its trip to Sicily. The two friends followed the long, jolting corridor of the express in motion. The restaurant-car was noisy and gaily lit. The abstract, shapeless country landscape flashed swiftly past the darkened windows, framing the beautiful oval face of Marcella Arteni.

Luigi was the first to reach her table:

'My dear Signorina Arteni, I excuse myself again for my small professional mistake. It's so easy to confuse journalism and police procedure!'

'Of course, Signor Commendatore,' replied the girl in blue mischievously. 'I like you so much. I tell you I am returning to Rome with my father, so when you meet me on the Palermo train you have every right to arrest me, but instead you excuse yourself gallantly... and I'm still free!'

'Allow me to return your compliment by saying that I admire your frankness, which I'm not crass enough to label "brazen impudence." Perhaps some day I shall be able to explain to you why I had to delay your arrest so enigmatically.'

At this point, his friend attempted without success to change the subject of the conversation, which irritated Luigi, who usually tried to conceal what he was trying to discover behind jocular remarks. Nevertheless, he tried to continue in the same merry vein:

'Please try to help me to entertain the young lady, instead of protesting. I understand that you are gaping in awe at her grace, but....'

She smiled at Luigi, but also at his gaping, awe-struck friend. Possibly at that moment she preferred Giorgio's silence to Luigi's words.

'So it appears that, as usual, I will speak for all of us,' laughed Luigi.

And he began to narrate the trip to Sicily he had made at the age of fifteen. Sicily had made a strong impression on the teenager: the titanic ruins of Selinunte; the suffused and quiet Monreale cathedral, so different from the garish Monreale of the art books; the splendid, serene, soft silence of San Giovanni degli Eremiti's cloisters; and that masterpiece of bulwarks, Eurialo Castle, still protecting for ever and ever the Arethusa of the Greek coins....

The train slowed, and an attendant announced that the restaurant-car would soon have to be uncoupled at Agropoli.

Luigi stood up with a gentle bow to Marcella:

'I'm going to buy some cigarettes, Giorgio. We shall meet back in our compartment. I leave you to your happy flirting, in the hope that you won't talk too much about the murder!'

Giorgio and Marcella remained silent, but their eyes were clearly following Luigi's instructions. Marcella broke the silence with a smile:

'Your friend is very nice!'

Giorgio nodded as a good friend, even if it wasn't very easy courting a girl whilst speaking about another man:

'Otherwise he wouldn't be my best friend!'

'You have a very good opinion of your friends... and of yourself,' smiled Marcella.

Giorgio began to speak about himself through his friendship with Luigi, hoping that Signorina Arteni was very interested in the former and not so much in the latter. And he felt he was right, so he started to question her about herself:

'Do you live in Rome?'

'Yes.'

'Near the station?'

'No.'

'Out by Porta Pia?'

'Not there either.'

He was trying to make her simile about his haphazard attempts to satisfy his own curiosity. He had hoped she would ask why he thought she would live there and not elsewhere, but Signorina Arteni answered curtly, almost angrily. So he admitted defeat:

'Really, I don't know where I would find you!'

He waited in vain for an answer. That jarring note had created a sudden, embarrassed coolness between them, possibly because it reminded them that their relationship was very superficial. Any conversation now seemed impossible: either too casual or too intimate.

But their mutual silence kept them close, almost reducing the distance between them on its own. So they stayed silently close to each other whilst the train kept running, and running, and running between the dark-blue sea, glittering with white-spangled sprays and stars, and the dark brown bulwark of the mountains, glittering with the pale yellow lights of remote and sparsely populated villages.

But the train stopped at Sapri, and the sudden, garish lights of the station divided them with a new, jarring jolt.

Vallesi returned to the compartment he shared with Luigi and found him half-asleep in a corner.

Giorgio was happy, uncannily happy, and he didn't know why. Certainly not because of Marcella's words nor any encouragement about future prospects. But he was in the mood where future prospects had no meaning, no meaning at all. He simply knew he loved Marcella as he'd never loved any woman before, and he'd just spent an hour alone in her company.

Renzi had returned to his compartment through the jolting, rumbling corridors of the train. As he was passing through the *wagon-lit*, the dark-blue clad conductor had called out to him:

'Excuse me, are you Signor Sabelli?'

Renzi was jolted, and not just because of the train, but he answered casually:

'No, why?'

He showed his official card to overcome the conductor's hesitation.

'Commendatore Renzi, could you follow me, please?'

He opened the door of one of the compartments with his passkey. In the feeble blue light Renzi could see two unoccupied berths.

'It's because of this suitcase, Signor Commendatore.'

He showed him a nondescript fibre suitcase, with a tag tied to the handle bearing the name of Giuseppe Sabelli. It was the same suitcase Boldrin had shown to Renzi, but....

'This berth was booked to Palermo.'

'What about the suitcase?' asked Renzi anxiously.

'It was placed on the bed by a gentleman just as the train was ready to go. He told me that berth number 5 had been booked by his friend Sabelli, and he wished to place the suitcase on the berth because Sabelli had been delayed and would arrive at the very last moment.'

'And this gentleman was...'

'Short, very fat, bald-headed, and apparently in a great hurry,' explained the attendant.

'With a bizarre rounded profile, almost mirroring the curve of the skull?' asked Renzi insistently, while smiling at the goofy image he'd evoked with his own words.

'Yes, yes,' confirmed attendant eagerly. 'Almost chinless, with a crooked nose.'

He was obviously describing Giovanni Marchetti, Sabelli's travelling companion. But Renzi wasn't satisfied: there was a jarring note, almost a jarring *leitmotif* in the story, and he had a curious, subconscious feeling. Unfortunately, he didn't have the right number of detectives on hand to shadow every passenger of that fatal flight.... Soon, he would have a far more tragic and gripping reason to complain.Meanwhile, the conductor was continuing his curious narration:

'I immediately placed the suitcase on the luggage rack—.'

'The traveller himself had no luggage?'

'An almost identical suitcase, if I remember correctly. Afterwards, I was too busy with the other passengers to keep track... but I checked half an hour ago and the compartment was still empty.'

'The other berth hadn't been booked?'

'No.'

'And was the suitcase still in its place?'

'Nobody could have got in, because I'd locked the door with my special key. But I noticed that nobody had claimed it, and that the compartment was still unoccupied. Even if the passenger had been in the restaurant-car, now....'

But Renzi was focused on the suitcase, quite certain that his memory wouldn't be wrong about a very small detail. He pulled a handful of skeleton keys from his pocket and pushed the mildly protesting conductor to one side. After several attempts he found the correct key and opened the suitcase.

Veiled by a small film of sawdust, Sabelli's eyes looked blindly out at the assistant commissioner.

'May I speak with Commissario Boldrin? This is Vice Questore Renzi... thank you... .Boldrin? I'm phoning from Sapri Station... Please tell me, have your detectives found Marchetti? He's on the Rome train? And does he have a suitcase with him? Thanks... So he left his companion's suitcase on the Palermo train. Yes, he was delayed and he asked his friend to place the suitcase on the train... His friend booked a berth, but didn't claim it for a very good reason... Worse, he has been murdered; his head and his arms are in the suitcase. Yes, yes, sawn or cut off, of course! I don't know anything more, the suitcase was full of sawdust... Yes, try to find Marchetti, he must be arriving in Rome about now... You can speak to my assistant, Vice Commissario Galbiati. Do you really think so? Frankly, I envy your confidence, my dear Boldrin. As for me, I have my doubts! Yes, yes, do what you have to do, of course, it's your case. I've left the poor man's remains with the station constabulary. I've detained the conductor, but really, I don't think that... No, I'm going to Palermo, of course. It's not the case that... Quite the contrary! Yes, the case is yours until my return, and I will be in Naples again as soon as I can. No, now's certainly not the time to lose them. I'll keep an eye on them, don't worry! Of course, not a single word to the newspapers here. I'm providing for it myself! Now I must really go, the train is leaving, I'll call you again tomorrow, hoping we can see some daylight... Good luck, Boldrin, and I'm wishing it for myself, too!'

Villa San Giovanni. Half-asleep, Luigi was vaguely conscious of the long stop and of the noisy manoeuvres whilst the train was being guided onto the ferry. He couldn't get to sleep again. By nightfall he'd stopped out of sheer drowsiness, but the shuddering images, created by his morbid fantasy and excited by his horrifying discovery, were in full possession of his mind now, and they were both shrieking and creepily insinuating. He'd tried every way to fight against them, but the horrible new fact created by its sudden, brisk appearance a veritable jumble of fantastic hypothesis, whereas the current situation demanded cool, calm logic and a reasonable replacing of the labels attached in Naples to the various characters of this creepy and mysterious play. But now that sleep was no longer a remedy, Luigi's fantasies were working overtime, so that when a slight rocking movement informed him that the boat was now leaving the shore, he decided to go into the corridor, where he found Marcella Arteni. He invited her to come to the deck and he helped her to navigate the very narrow passage between the train's cars and the engine-room. As they were climbing the iron stairway, Luigi wryly complimented her:

'I never thought that an early bird could catch a beautiful girl.' Sure to have found the right diversion for his attack, he included in a sweeping gesture the splendid landscape and Marcella kissed by the early sun:

'And Giorgio is asleep and missing this magnificent view!'

Miss Arteni smiled but seemed to prefer dedicating herself humbly to the landscape: Messina was a bunch of little white dice on the short, flat coastline with, on its right side, the lighthouse and a triangle of mountains, hidden amongst the darker clouds and barely pierced by dawn's early light. Behind it, the coast lost itself in the mist, becoming almost indistinguishable, blending and confusing itself with the Aspromonte. After a long, awe-struck viewing, Miss Arteni decided to at least accept the compliment with another radiant smile:

'If you can enjoy my company this morning you must thank my mother.'

'Really?' replied Luigi, with a sort of incredulous satisfaction.

'My mother loves Messina, and she taught me never to lose this moment of the voyage. So I always watch the Stretto from the deck... It's really marvellous at dawn!'

But Luigi appeared absent-minded, lost in his mysterious thoughts. In the brief silence which followed, he touched lightly on Signorina Arteni's hand, in simple, happy, thoughtless enjoyment:

'If this were a French novel, they would write about couples, side by side, leaning on the railings,' he said, smilingly indicating another pair of heads leaning out to view the sea, just like them.

'But...?' she replied immediately, ready for the sting in the tail.

'But they are near, and we are so distant. We can notice them, and they notice only themselves.'

'Are you envious of them?'

'Is that a question?'

She was taken aback by his remark, and she immediately found a barb for her playful revenge:

'Can you give me some kind advice, Dr. Renzi?'

'I will hear you with pleasure as soon as I can, but as you can see we are soon to disembark in Messina and I'm very sorry to have to leave you alone, just for a couple of moments.'

Whilst the boat was being tied to the wharf, he jumped out and ran to the Marine Station office. After a couple of minutes there, he ran back towards the departing train and smiled merrily at Marcella, who was helping him to jump on the wagon:

'And now, let's hear your request for kind advice.' He smiled again, with affectionate satisfaction.

'Actually, it's a warning, not really a request for advice, and it can sound quite ominous. The classic mystery novel sleuth has the very bad habit of falling in love with the beautiful girl he was supposed to arrest.'

'Obviously. She's always innocent. Beautiful girls can never be guilty. Not in my book. But in this particular case, I haven't the slightest intention of falling for a beautiful, innocent girl.'

'Thank you so much,' she replied sardonically, as if she'd been hurt in some way by his jocular remarks, but Luigi touched her arm again gently:

'No, please, I'm serious. Don't try to find a mysterious secret in my words, or any inappropriate and very vulgar innuendo. I'm simply speaking on a third person's behalf....'

The young woman blushed with confusion at her sudden understanding of his demeanour, so Luigi rushed to add, in a less serious tone:

'Don't think too badly of me, please. But I now know the exact reason for your trip to Palermo.'

She fluttered her long lashes briefly:

'How?'

'I phoned the Hotel des Palmes, just before my risky climb onto this wretched train. Your words had made me think and understand, you know.'

There was a moment of suspenseful incertitude, then Signorina Arteni smiled admiringly at him and offered her hand:

'Friends?'

'Friends.'

Luigi returned the handshake and the smile with pleasure:

'The friends of our friends are our friends, isn't that what they say?'

6-PALERMO

Two taxicabs were following each other on the long, straight avenue from the railway station to the Hotel des Palmes. In the first was the girl in blue, and in the second her faithful follower, the reporter. So far, the latter had only managed to exchange a few frosty words with her. When they had parted, her frank smile had been directed at Renzi, and Renzi only. But Giorgio thought he'd detected a tinge of bitterness, of defeat. Luigi was a good talker and she liked him very much, but she wasn't pleased about his increasingly distant attitude. He hadn't been imposing himself; he'd been paving the way for someone else, and the girl in blue reasoned that the only person who could be grateful about his sacrifice would be his friend Giorgio himself. Yet Giorgio was cursing his own stupidity. He didn't even know the girl's hotel in Palermo! Which is why he'd been reduced to squalid taxi-shadowing, as in all those bad old films....

Certainly, he was trying to solve the Great Flying Boat Mystery on behalf of his paper, *La Gazzetta*, and Marcella Arteni was one of the prime suspects... But he had to admit cockily to himself that she was the only Dornier passenger he had any intention of following.

More seriously, he acknowledged that he didn't actually know the part she'd played in that dark, obscure mystery. Up until now, he'd subconsciously dismissed any suspicion he might have had about her, but now that idea was returning more and more insistently, he had to face up to it. But now the taxi ahead had stopped and the girl in blue was entering Hotel Des Palmes with her customary grace, whilst the wicked idea slipped once again from Vallesi's mind.

He waited patiently for several minutes, and when the girl came out of the hotel, he rushed to enter, happy to notice the total emptiness of the reception area. He approached the bell-boy standing in front of the elevator.

'Please, about the girl who just went out a couple of minutes ago.'

He had been prepared to show his reporter's card and adopt the classic policeman's attitude, but the view of an inviting coin was far more persuasive to the young lad, already sheepishly confused by the brisk, authoritative tone of Giorgio's voice:

'Are you a real detective?'

'Yes, yes. Where did she go?'

'She asked me about a lady, and when I told her she was on an excursion to Pellegrino Mountain, she asked me where she could find a cab....'

Giorgio fought fiercely with the revolving door as he rushed out of the hotel. He cursed himself for not having kept his taxi. He made uncertain steps in all directions as he tried to find one and at last a garage beckoned to him from a street corner. Of course, no girl in blue had rented a car from them, but Vallesi was at least able to find a taxi for his trip up Pellegrino Mountain.

Giorgio looked in vain along the road climbing up the dreary, barren mountain, only sparsely covered by a pale film of fading grass. They hadn't seen a car in either direction. The motor of the 521, pushed at full speed, was labouring breathlessly up the steep incline. It seemed very odd that Marcella would have gone so far, up to the peak of the mountain... Anxious and feeling deceived, Giorgio continued to peer at the asphalt strip covered and uncovered at the mountain's madcap whim. We can only share his despair and his total neglect of the wonderful natural landscape, until he reached the small, deserted square where the road ended. He looked around with even greater despair, towards a long rounded canyon in which white rubble was unenthusiastically tracing a continuation.

To the left of the small square, a drive had been cut across the rocky flank of the mountain, swiftly disappearing behind its powerful ribs.

A group of five or six people had assembled in the Palermo Alpine Club Hotel at the peak of Pellegrino Mountain. Vallesi scanned the gorgeous, flamboyant party of visitors attentively. Needless to say, Marcella wasn't amongst them, but possibly the mysterious lady she had sought at the Hotel Des Palmes was, unless the bell-boy had been lying or joking. Giorgio was an incorrigible optimist, however, and he confidently trusted the eager lad.

A slim young man was standing apart from the group in brooding silence. He was light-haired, with a sort of laziness in his clear, wide face. In stark contrast, a scarlet-lipped young woman was the centre of the group. She was very attractive, with a finely-chiselled, sensual face and a softly curved nose that was vaguely Jewish. The girl was a bundle of energy: breezy, jolly and very lively.

The light-haired young man was following her every movement with a lingering jealousy, particularly when she exploded in throaty laughter. Far luckier than he was the man who was verbally skirmishing with her, enthusiastically. He was in his forties, broad-shouldered and very good-looking, with a youngish face under a shock of grey hair.

Next to them stood a tall, slender blonde lady, who, despite her rosy freshness, was fighting desperately against encroaching middle age. Her companion was a younger and even nervier man, animating the general conversation with his briskly staccato words. He made a sudden appeal to all those outside:

'Ladies and gentlemen, aren't we going to sign the guest register?'

The hotel manager, like a faithful conjuror's assistant, hastened to display it. Giorgio was the last to sign, so he casually took note of the other names: Lucilio and Miriam d'Alfedena were certainly the lazy young gentleman and his small, breezy wife. The blonde lady had signed in as Gianna Arteni Morello, which prompted Giorgio to think suddenly about Marcella. They were certainly very much alike, so she must have been her—.

He threw the pen down and rushed outside again. The slender girl in blue was emerging from the drive.

'Mother!'

'Dear Marcella,' replied the aging blonde beauty in astonishment.

Giorgio was not disappointed, but certainly he would have chosen a far more adventurous ending for his escapade. After all, he was in the midst of a family reunion, with no possible role to play in it. He was about to head back to Palermo to prepare a new attack on the girl, but she had noticed him already and she acknowledged his presence with her customary frostiness, having only the power to pull him forward, as if attracted by an ice magnet.

'Good morning, Marcella!'

'Good morning, Signor Vallesi.'

After another frosty silence, she introduced him to her mother with a bored remoteness, bordering on fatigue:

'Mother, this is Signor Vallesi of *La Gazzetta*, a casual travel acquaintance.'

Giorgio bowed and, uttering a couple of vague words, suddenly found himself alone in the icy void, as the girl in blue dragged her mother away by the arm.

Luigi Renzi emerged from the Palermo Police Headquarters after a long meeting with the high commissioner. He took an avenue which descended gently towards the blue sea, its shining sparkle enhanced by the incoming twilight. Keeping to the left, he walked in the direction of the Quattro Canti, where he was due to meet Vallesi. He stopped at a newsstand:

'May I have today's newspaper?'

'Here it is, *La Ora*!'

'Do you have any of the Rome or Milan papers?'

'We have *Il Corriere* and *La Gazzetta del Popolo*.'

'I'll have *Il Corriere*, thanks.'

A swift perusal of the paper didn't reveal any details of the creepy findings on the Palermo train. Renzi was still reading *Il Corriere* when Vallesi appeared from the direction of the Via Maqueda. Luigi smiled at him, flourishing the paper:

'Did you know that your friend was a "young and promising police detective"?'

But his friend was clearly not in the mood for a joke.

Luigi tried to guess the reason for his discomfort:

'Had an argument with your would-be future mother-in-law?'

'I beg your pardon?'

'Marcella's mother.'

'How did you know? Ah, if you really did know....'

'Do I know or don't I? I know, I know, believe me, I know.'

'What do you know? And why didn't you tell me about it?'

Luigi was a bit stunned by his friend's new violence. He had never been the brutal kind, far from it! Asking himself about his clearly trying experience, he tried to explain calmly and quietly: *I'm lost, is that supposed to mean something?*

'Sorry, I haven't had the time or the opportunity. I only guessed the reason for Marcella's trip to Palermo this morning. She had told me about her mother's frequent trips to Sicily, and I remembered that her father never mentioned his dear wife when he recovered his daughter from our claws. But Marcella spoke about a very lively and loving mother, no doubt about it, so I guessed that her parents' relationship wasn't all it could be. In any case, it was one of the more plausible reasons for Marcella's sudden trip and her father's swift expedition to Naples, hot on her heels, to take her back to Rome with him. So, it needed to be checked out, didn't it? I phoned the Hotel Des Palmes, the only suitable establishment in Palermo for a travelling Signora Arteni. And I was lucky, as you know.'

Vallesi was himself again, so Luigi could add impertinently:

'If you hadn't rushed away so quickly… But it's far better to have checked out the splendid correctness of my deductions…as you did at your own expense, it seems, when you followed her in a taxi….'

Vallesi's only answer was a smile, but his friend pressed him to narrate his own sad experience, taking him by the elbow and steering him along via Maqueda. Giorgio felt ashamed of himself as he thought about his demeaning meeting with the Arteni women. Only when he had ended his tale did he become his jocular self again:

'So, as you see, we can strike Marcella from the list of suspects.'

'That's the third name I've cancelled today. The first was Larini: our teller duly forwarded his documents and he's returning to Rome on the three o'clock train today.'

'But that doesn't matter at all. The only important thing was his sudden departure from the flying boat!'

'A circumstance with no particular relevance. The reason for his sudden flight has been confirmed, and we have nothing else against him, I'm afraid,' explained Luigi, with a sort of tired exasperation.

But Giorgio was still unaware of the tragic discovery on the Palermo express, so he had fully regained his own usual thoughtless gaiety, as if he were actually reading an exciting mystery novel:

'And the third name you scratched from the list? It wouldn't be our lady in red, by any chance?'

'No, although we shall speak about her soon enough. It was Pagelli-Bertieri. He did indeed leave for Tunis, just as he told us.'

'I hope you alerted the local police!'

'Of course, but I'm quite certain that he'll simply forward his letter, just as Larini did.'

Suddenly he remembered a detail he'd noticed previously, which had slipped his mind immediately afterwards. Pagelli had noted Marcella's anxiety after the banker's disappearance had been noticed. She'd asked the name of the vanished financier several times. It wasn't very significant in and of itself, but even if he tried not to remember the tragic discovery of the night before, even if he thought that the culprit was probably now in the hands of the police, a possibly excessive scruple was pushing him to solve that tiny, unimportant little mystery as well. So he gripped his friend's elbow and dragged him along via Stabile to the Hotel des Palmes.

'Look, Giorgio, if we know very well why Marcella is in Palermo, we have a ninety per cent chance that her anxiety on the plane was caused by her mother's trip to Sicily.' He tried desperately to smile again. 'So I'm giving you the chance to meet your future mother-in-law again.'

Giorgio didn't react to his jest at all, so Luigi asked more solemnly:

'So you really are serious about her?'

But Vallesi remained silent.

'So, when you meet Marcella again, you can always put the blame on your silly friend and on his stupid way of muddling everything up.... '

At the Hotel des Palmes, they couldn't find either the mother or the daughter. But the highly cooperative hotel manager gave Luigi every possible detail about a group which had arrived in Palermo with Gianna Arteni a couple of days before. They were joining her on a Mediterranean cruise on a yacht owned by the British banker Rowsett. Apart from Gianna and Rowsett himself, the group included the other people Vallesi had seen on Pellegrino Mountain: Lucilio and Miriam D'Alfedena, and M. le Comte d'Espinade.'

'As you can see, our puzzle is recomposing itself,' observed Renzi, once they were out of the hotel. 'And every new piece is demonstrating the innocence of all the people on board the plane! If it seemed materially impossible that they could have had any part in the banker's vanishing act, we could at least have suspected them of some very clever trick... but now.... ' He stopped for a moment, trying to find some optimistic energy in the same pessimistic words he was saying. 'So,' he continued, with a sort of nervous excitement, 'I really can't choose amongst the three possible options: an impossible murder, an impossible suicide and an impossible accident! Everything is materially and psychologically impossible! Look at your brilliant sleuth of a friend, look how "the young hope of Italian police," so praised by this very clever newspaper is so reduced!'

He crumpled the pages nervously, until his friend managed to rescue them from total destruction:

'If you hate it so much, at least leave me the chance to read it!'

He restored the newspaper's moral and physical integrity and he searched and found the Flying Boat Mystery item, so Luigi was obliged to walk nervously, his hands in pockets, around the lamplight where his friend had stopped to read. At last, the latter lifted his head from the half-crumpled paper:

'It seems that my colleague does not completely share your doubts. He firmly excludes the murder and accident options, and plumps for a desperate suicide solution!'

'Very good reasoning, the clever fellow! Certainly there's no need to ask him how Agliati could have committed suicide through that wretched skylight.' Renzi seemed calmer and happier now. 'And it's not necessary to tell you that you must not use in any way my strictly personal confidences. But you'll be the first to be informed of any new developments, don't worry!'

'The usual deal between sleuth and reporter, you can find it in any good mystery novel,' smiled Vallesi.

Giorgio was still casually reading the newspaper in silence, when he grasped his friend's arm:

'Look here, Luigi, this is interesting....'

THE FLYING BOAT MYSTERY AGAIN
VANISHING BANKER'S WIFE IS GOING TO ITALY

Athens, the Thirteenth of....(as phoned by our local correspondent)

Maria Agliati, wife of famous banker Francesco Agliati, who vanished from a flying boat on the 12th, during the Ostia-Naples flight, is leaving on the Ausonia to Brindisi with her daughter Alice. They will arrive tomorrow in the evening and they will direct themselves immediately to Rome.

'Yesterday's news, so they will arrive this evening,' commented Renzi. 'And tomorrow afternoon they will be in Rome. Another good reason to phone Galbiati.'

He dragged Vallesi to Police Headquarters, to the high commissioner's bureau.

'I was trying to reach you at your hotel, Dr. Renzi....'

'Any news?'

'Regarding the Martellis... The detective shadowing them has discovered a connection with some very fishy people....'

Hoping for a long-awaited break, Giorgio and Luigi exchanged very interested looks.

'Investigatore Agosti reported that the Martellis had immediately gone to a sordid hotel near to the station, the Italia, and had immediately made a phone call from the cabin in the hall, even before going up to their rooms. After they finished their very long call, Agosti was able to check with the switchboard that they had called a lawyer named Alfredini, a suspicious character we have had under strict observation for some time, hoping to be able to grill him at the first possible opportunity. His office had been a thriving concern some years ago, but he gambled away his reputation on the market and on the green table. Stocks and cards were his thirst and his damnation. He lost trust, fame and customers, but as of today, he's still dealing with certain companies very interested in the new industrial development areas of Corleone and Piana dei Greci.'

'Shady businesses, needless to say.'

'Very, very shady, but without any legal evidence of certifiable crookedness. If only this time we could transform our suspicions into solid proofs... It would be very good news, very good news indeed!'

Vallesi smiled, thinking that Alfredini certainly wouldn't be sharing that hope. In the meantime, a phone call from Agosti was passed through to the high commissioner and the two friends looked expectantly at the new developments:

'Yes, I understand. 41, via Papireto... Yes, of course, we're leaving now and will be there in ten minutes....'

The police car drove rapidly to via Papireto, where they could make out detective Agosti as an ominous shadow in a dark courtyard in front of shady Alfredini's house.

Renzi was a bit embarrassed by his own presence at the stake-out, but the high commissioner reassured him:

'Don't worry, Dr. Renzi, we haven't very much regard for this Alfredini fellow. A fishy individual, indeed! And he knows very well our opinion of him, and would, if he could, have escaped abroad ages ago, believe me!'

Their official raid left the manservant speechless and devoid of protest.

A strip of light filtered below the door of one of the rooms. After a tense eavesdropping, the high commissioner whispered:

'He's doing one of his tricks. He's praising a certain big deal too much... It's our cue, follow me!'

He knocked briefly on the door, opened it and he found himself in front of four people around a desk: the Martellis, Alfredini, and a big man with a sort of brazen self-important arrogance. Vallesi immediately noticed the parcel of stocks and shares on the big square desk. He had passed six painful months of his youth among these garish filigree-paper documents....

'Up to your usual tricks, Signor Alfredini?' asked the police chief.

Alfredini nodded, as he was uncertain about the other's demeanour. In the absence of a reaction, the high commissioner pursued his heavily ironic attack:

'Could you explain this very winning deal to us as well?' He indicated the stocks and shares to the stuttering lawyer. 'I have so much trust in you that I could almost buy some shares myself... Almost, only almost, of course!'

'You could be very lucky, it's really a big deal! The SFASO shares, issued by the Company for the Agricultural Development of Western Sicily, are very safe and highly rewarding....'

Giorgio approached the stocks on the desk. He was remembering something... He turned a share over and observed the violet stamp on it:

'This is the option stamp, isn't it? Privileged shares?'

Alfredini confirmed grudgingly:

'For its 25th anniversary, SFASO issued a special privileged option share with a bonus of one free share for every three shares purchased....'

'They've been rising, haven't they?'

'From 520 to 545, so far, and they will continue rising until the offer is ended.'

The Martellis were silent. Even the overbearing Signora Martelli had had to absorb her surprise at the police raid before intervening in the argument with her usual belligerent acrimony:

'Now that we have persuaded these gentlemen, can we return to our business deal: we've agreed on 530, I believe?'

Alfredini had now absorbed the impact of the intrusion, and was recovering far faster than the two flying boat passengers; he even permitted himself a little dignified peevishness when he answered acridly:

'Impossible, my dear lady, utterly and totally impossible! Quite ridiculous, indeed! I ask you, dear Commendatore, how could I sell for 530 such highly rewarding, highly remunerative, successfully rising stocks I obtained at.... ' But his voice became less and less persuasive while he tried to follow the whispered conversation between Giorgio and Renzi, in a far corner of the room.

Now, on cue, the two actors were assuming centre stage:

'Commendatore, we are hereby stopping a big fraud,' announced Renzi. 'My friend Vallesi is a banking expert and he can explain the trick with far more competent details, but basically we can say, if I understand it correctly, that SFASO issued two series of stocks, the privileged option shares, giving bonus rights and now reaching a value of 545; and the common shares, not giving any options or bonus rights and reaching only a teeny-weeny 525. The stocks on the desk, for example, having nothing to do with any options, apart from a very fake violet stamp on the back.'

Alfredini jumped out of the shadows and into the dark corridor, but after a shrill whistle from the police chief, and a moment of even more anxious waiting, a small confusion in the hall announced the triumphant arrival of the officers, one of whom appeared in the door frame:

'Gotcha!'

This time the Martellis were really and truly petrified. The events were too much even for Signora Martelli's venomous tongue. Even when the high commissioner, after a few words of officious reproach, announced severely that they were free to leave, they couldn't shake off their astonishment, and only when the house was free of its intruders did they sleep-walk out of it, into the street of their defeat and discomfort.

Giorgio was still stunned and lost in thought:

'So this was the motive for their sudden rush to Palermo,' he commented at last.

'Of course,' smiled the very satisfied high commissioner. 'I'm very grateful to you, dear colleague.' He smiled at Luigi. 'Your coming to Palermo permitted me to nail a crook I'd had my eye on for many months. I've waited ages for this chance, but somehow I don't think that Alfredini will be quite as happy about your timely intervention.'

His self-satisfied laughter died in the silence. Giorgio noticed that his friend was worried, particularly when he threw back his head as he so often did to indicate a sort of thoughtless determination.

Back at the police HQ, Renzi immediately phoned his office in Rome.

'Is that you, Galbiati?'

'Yes, sir.'

'Did you receive Commissario Boldrin's communication?'

'I have the situation completely in hand, Dr. Renzi.'

'Good. Did you arrest Marchetti when he arrived at the Termini Station?'

'Yes sir. And with his suitcase full of human parts....'

'His suitcase as well? Was he walking merrily along with it?'

'Yes, with the armless and legless torso inside. The limbs had been very professionally sawn off.'

'What does Marchetti have to say for himself?'

'He seemed surprised when we arrested him. He was more angry than scared about the accusation, but he seemed utterly astonished and terrified once we opened the suitcase.'

'But he admits that it's his suitcase?'

'Yes, sir.'

'Yet he still claims to be innocent?'

'Absolutely. After the first moment of astonishment, he began to claim, with a poker face and a vigorous and totally fake indignation that—.'

'His poker face doesn't match too well with his stupidity. God, he fell quite blindly and childishly into a very simple trap... What's he saying now?'

'According to him, he lost his friend Sabelli immediately after their release from Naples police. Sabelli stayed in a phone booth for some minutes....'

'And so we can't check on it, very good for him....'

'Then he asked Marchetti to take his suitcase, and to wait for him in the hall of the railway station until half-past six. He had previously booked a berth by phone on the night express to Palermo. If he were to be delayed, Marchetti was asked to take Sabelli's suitcase into the train compartment with him, before his train left from Naples to Rome.'

'And so how did the grisly body parts end up in his own suitcase?'

'He can offer many protests, but no explanation at all!'

'Any clues in the suitcase?'

'No. We found the victim's coat and waistcoat wrapped in a corner, but unfortunately the pockets had been emptied with great care.'

'Did you notice the blue airline label on the suitcase?'

'No, but I can look for it, if you want. And you, Dr.Renzi? How did you fare in Palermo?'

'Very badly, thanks. Tomorrow, very possibly, I will return to Rome.'

'With a short stop in Naples?'

'You know me too well, Galbiati. But for a single day only, I hope. Do you know that Signora Agliati is coming to Rome? Please, go to meet her, she'll arrive tomorrow in the early afternoon, and I don't think I can be there... Please try to question her immediately... saving her in the meantime from reporters' curiosity!'

'As you wish, sir. Don't worry.'

'Any news about her husband?'

'Only that he lived in Italy until 1917, then he expatriated to Greece and founded the Italy & Greece Bank in Athens. In 1918, he became a Greek citizen....'

'Good, and before his leaving for Greece?'

'There's no information about him whatsoever. Isn't it possible that Agliati could be an alias, a name he assumed in Greece?'

'And why would he have done such a thing?'

'I don't know, it's only an impression, but his sudden leaving during the war, his immediate change of nationality... it sounds so mystifying, doesn't it?'

'Why not? Dear Galbiati, that's something we have to investigate. Now, where was he staying during his last visit to Rome?'

'At the D'Azeglio Hotel, but my investigation there yielded no results at all. He arrived at four p.m. on the eleventh and immediately ran some errands. He returned for dinner and remained in the hotel until the next morning, then departed again at half-past eight, leaving his luggage in reception with orders to send it immediately to the Port of Brindisi Marine Railway Station. He returned to the hotel at ten o'clock to settle his bill and collect the luggage shipment receipt. After, he—.'

'Very good, Galbiati. Where is the airline bus terminal to Ostia?'

'In Largo Tritone. The bus leaves at ten a.m.'

'Please ask the Brindisi railway police for the luggage.'

'Done. I asked them to send it to Boldrin, in Naples.'

'Well done, dear Galbiati, well done! Did you follow my instructions about the crew?'

'Of course, sir.'

'They will be grounded by SANA with no permission to leave?'

'Grounded and collared as of yesterday evening, sir.'

'Well then, I have really nothing more to ask. Goodbye, dear Galbiati.'

'Good luck, sir.'

After the call, Renzi commented to Vallesi:

'Galbiati is a good man, but even from him we have no news, no news at all!'

The following morning, he repeated the same depressing phrase to Vallesi. They were lunching in the railway station restaurant, after a very short visit by Renzi to Signora Antonini and her mysterious daughter.

Luigi had been introduced by an elderly maid in black-and-white into a vaguely Spanish sitting room. Vanna Ferrari entered the darkened room, clad in a violet dress, clearly cut to fit far older shoulders. Renzi immediately got to the point:

'Signora Ferrari, you left your husband suddenly....'

Her tale was quite long and tempestuous, but luckily Renzi had a quiet ear, trained by years of experience, and he could calm and soothe her in the more heated and fierce passages. Signora Ferrari was not a wife. Her husband was quite a bad lot: jealous, violent, possessive, and ultimately unfaithful. Having had proof of his marital infidelity, she had faced his last brutal outburst of jealousy with a new confidence, during a very violent explosion of bridal resentment on the morning of the 12th. Her husband's answer was, of course, no less violent and spiteful. She threatened to leave him for good, he defied her to do so, and she did it. The day before, she had been clad in a green-emerald evening dress and had left her pocketbook in the matching lizard-green bag. She grabbed it with a sudden total disdain for elegance and fashion and made her violent and spiteful door-slamming exit into via Tritone, where she immediately looked for a taxi, but saw instead the blue SANA bus stopped at the via Crispi corner. She thought that a flying boat would be a very swift and effective way to escape from an odious husband. Certainly, he would have searched for her everywhere, but a plane flight would have quite successfully eluded his mean and miserly imagination.

'When I arrived at my mother's home,' she concluded triumphantly, 'I found two cables from him, asking after me, and you can imagine my mother's intervention on his behalf.' She smiled with a sort of acrid, ironic tenderness and then sealed her scarlet lips. Luigi returned her ironic and tender smile, sure as he was that a sudden arrival of Ferrari to Palermo would very easily have the requested results.

Her mother's moral persuasion would have no need at all to be exerted! So Luigi could return to his investigation, and to his failure.

Giorgio and Luigi were walking again on a station platform. Very unusually they were silent, having really nothing to say. They were both so baffled by the mystery that they were waiting in desperate hope of a break.

'Are you staying in Palermo?' asked Renzi at last.

'I will leave at half past five this afternoon.'

Renzi had one foot on the carriage steps:

'OK, have a nice trip and give my love to Marcella!'

7-A BODY AND TOO MANY SUITCASES

Renzi saluted Chief Inspector Boldrin warmly as he entered his bureau:

'Here we are again, sooner than we thought!'

Boldrin lifted himself up from his chair with the usual tired exertion, and shook hands with a marked lack of enjoyment. He tried not to fall over the many items of luggage encumbering the room. Renzi thought about asking jokingly if he had put in for a transfer to a better bureau, but Boldrin's gloomy face caused him to drop the idea.

'Have you found the two other suitcases?' he asked instead, more solemnly.

'They found them the other morning on the train from Naples to Brindisi.' He read the obvious question in Renzi's eyes and nodded grudgingly. 'Yes, with the usual grisly remains in them.... '

'Same victim, of course? '

'Of course. The train police couldn't give us a single clue. I think that someone left the suitcases on the train at Naples station.'

'When did it leave Naples?'

'At 7.55 p.m.'

'So, exactly one hour and twenty-five minutes after the Palermo express.'

'And the suitcases were left on the train only a few minutes before departure. The Brindisi express experienced a long delay, due to minor repairs in one of the carriages, apparently.'

Renzi examined the four similar suitcases. Boldrin helped him, dividing them in three lots:

'Look, this is the one you found on the Palermo express, and these are the two found in Brindisi.... '

Renzi opened the Sicilian suitcase. Inside, it still had traces of sawdust and blood, but amongst all the bloodstains the famous mysterious numbers were still a remarkable sight:

8615915252241285   1519

He had not noticed them on the night of the eerie discovery, but he was reassured to see them again and smiled with a sort of satisfaction. But he smiled with even more satisfaction when Boldrin confirmed one of his predictions:

'I have something very odd to show you, Dr. Renzi... It's about those wretched numbers....'

He picked up one of the Brindisi suitcases, opened it and pointed to the lid. Inside, near to the hinges, with ironic neatness, someone had written a series of numbers with a violet pencil:

$$8615915252241285 \ 1519$$

Boldrin studied Renzi's face without noticing the least trace of the highly anticipated astonishment. Instead, the other was smiling with a vague irony at the ominous finding. He examined the two Brindisi suitcases—more on the outside than on the inside, curiously enough—and, when he stood up, seemed quite satisfied with his own mysterious and secretive thoughts.

'What does Marchetti say about the new suitcases?'

'Nothing at all. He denies everything. He denies having bought them in Naples, he denies having bought them in Rome, he denies having taken them with him on the plane.'

Renzi quite approved of both Marchetti's desperate defence and Boldrin's energetic accusations:

'Certainly he did it! It can't be otherwise! There's no doubt whatsoever, who else could it have...? Of course, he wasn't alone, he couldn't have....'

'Of course. The Brindisi suitcases were left on the train after Marchetti had already left for Rome almost an hour earlier!'

'So it was a premeditated, very well-organized crime, committed by two or more accomplices!'

'And these people,' smiled Luigi, 'must have also had prior knowledge of the sudden stop at Naples, when the plane was grounded and ended its flight....'

'... because of the mysterious banker Agliati's disappearance!' concluded Boldrin.

'So the two cases are very connected... but it's better that this connection be totally unknown to reporters and their adoring readers!'

'I have taken very effective measures, don't worry. Reporter interference is and will be banned and forbidden.' But Boldrin was anxious to return to the trail, almost fearful of losing his thread on the way: 'Don't you think that the connection between Sabelli's murder and Agliati's disappearance could be quite helpful?'

'Meaning it could clear up the vanishing banker case? Possibly, but not the way, the means actually used for the trick; just its form.'

'Its form?'

'This disappearance can only have three possible forms: murder, suicide, or accident. If Sabelli's killers were able to effectively predict the plane's stop in Naples in order to plan their crime, then two of our forms are certainly excluded, because it's impossible to forecast a suicide or an accident: an accident is, by definition, an unforeseen event, and a suicide is usually dependent on a sudden, depressing whim... human will is very variable, flighty and spontaneous, I'm afraid....'

Boldrin was immediately grasping and employing the logical terminology of his superior:

'So there remains the third form, murder!'

'But we never counted, possibly erroneously, a fourth hypothetical form, and it's a quite easily predictable one, because of its same wilful inevitability: the premeditated, extemporaneous or definitive disappearance of a running subject. In plain words, his escape or flight or fugue.'

The very theatrical exposition was followed by a brief silence:

'Do you think then that Agliati had intended to escape during the flight?'

'It's only a hypothesis, nothing more, dear Boldrin. I really don't know how or why Agliati could have so effectively and mysteriously performed his vanishing act. I'll never forgive myself if you take my random, blindfolded long shot seriously. Very possibly my hypothesis is very, very wrong. So we must leave our beautiful mystery novel rational reasoning about a very irrational and not so reasonable disappearance, and return to the more sordid and matter-of-fact reality of the Sabelli murder case. So we are, alas, passing from splendid, abstract theory to prosaic, ordinary and commonplace reality. We have duly handcuffed and jailed a very plausible if prosaic culprit who, unfortunately, has no intention whatsoever of confessing and admitting his heinous crime!'

Boldrin ignored Renzi's ironic amusement and quietly answered:

'That's where things stand. There's no doubt about his guilt, you're perfectly correct. No doubt whatsoever.'

But Renzi asked ironically:

'So, how we can reconstruct the murder, following the usual procedures, including means, opportunity, possible complicities, motives, alibis, and of course the extraordinary scene of the crime?'

Boldrin hesitated for a moment, then looked his boss in the eye, weighing his seriousness. After a brief hesitation, he decided to answer in a more serious and officious tone:

'I think that the crimes were organized and perpetrated by a powerful and numerous gang, possibly ruled, aided and abetted by the Italy & Argentina bank managers. Haven't we found a managing director's phone number in two of the infamous suitcases? '

Luigi nodded and Boldrin continued his train of thought more confidently: 'Our friend Marchetti was, of course, a gang member, and poor Sabelli too, even if he was possibly only a minor legman. I'm not seeing too clearly Pagelli-Bertieri's role, and very likely the bank teller Larini has no part at all in the whole affair, being only a casual bystander.'

He paused for a moment, but his superior made no comments or objections, so Boldrin continued:

'And, of course, Sabelli and Marchetti were on the plane in relation to Agliati's disappearance.... '

'Are you talking about a cause and effect kind of relationship? And, if so, how did it work, please?'

The poor chief inspector's thoughts were a bit shaken by the interruption, so Luigi dismissed it with a sweeping gesture of his hand:

'Very well, we can talk about that later... Please, continue.'

'We both agree that Agliati's disappearance was organized by the gang which stopped the plane so very effectively in Naples. The gang predicted and very possibly provoked the stop. Other members of the gang had been previously called to Naples. But during our questioning a totally unpredictable discovery disrupted their very carefully laid plans.'

'We found and correctly read the numbers on the suitcase's inner lining.'

'Correct. So we can only guess at their own trouble and dismay. Sabelli, I think, was only a minor accomplice who had no knowledge at all of the overall plan. When he eventually understood it, he became scared about it. He feared for his safety and possibly thought about a little blackmail of his own. So he fought bitterly and violently with his accomplices, who were then obliged to take the grisly measures we have seen afterwards.'

Renzi reflected in silence on the situation as Boldrin had described it.

'Certainly we are fighting against desperate and resourceful people, no doubt about it,' he murmured, almost to himself. 'How do you think Sabelli was murdered?'

Boldrin seemed a bit hurt and surprised by this superfluous, embarrassing question:

'Marchetti and the gang lured him into a trap, of course.'

Renzi didn't ask him where, but he was soon to get the dramatic, unrequested answer.

'They had an argument and Sabelli was killed ... It was a premeditated action, or possibly they tried to scare him off; he reacted with unexpected violence and the fight had a tragic and brutal ending. The problem was then how to hide the body and any other clues very quickly. They had Sabelli's and Marchetti's suitcases, and they bought another pair.... '

'Completely identical,' added Renzi.

'Of course. They sawed up the body and put the parts in the sawdust-filled suitcases. To divert suspicion, they booked a berth on the *wagon-lit* to Palermo, using Sabelli's name. As a cynical touch, Marchetti put his friend's suitcase on the Palermo train, inventing a phony errand requested by the man partially contained in his own luggage. The train conductor immediately read Sabelli's name on the suitcase tag... Afterwards, Marchetti quietly took the Rome train with his own suitcase. The other two were left by his accomplices on the Brindisi train, almost an hour later.'

Luigi waited for the echo of the chief inspector's words to die out, then observed:

'Dear Boldrin, there are a couple of holes in your reconstruction of the murderers' plan, possibly because the plan itself was flawed. Even though they were very resourceful and skilful killers, don't forget... Two were technical errors, and the third, far more serious and less explicable, was psychological. Beginning with the first two mistakes, you correctly noted that the four suitcases were completely alike: same factory, same kind of model... Twins of birth, twins of fate. But a single circumstance can divide them in two pairs: Sabelli's and Marchetti's suitcases were on the plane, and still have a memento of their flight: a blue airline tag pasted on the side. But the killers, thoughtful as they were, didn't think to make them disappear, even though they'd had the clever idea of writing on one of the newly-bought suitcases the same mysterious numbers we had found in Sabelli's, and of applying to their phony Sabelli's suitcase a leather tag with his name on it. And the blue labels' tiny clue can allow us to reconstruct very effectively the complex adventures of the two pairs of suitcases in Naples: the blue-labelled suitcases coming here by plane with their owners, and the new, unlabelled fakes by other means.'

Luigi paused for a moment, allowing poor old Boldrin the opportunity to absorb this very confusing luggage merry-go-round. When the chief inspector had at last grasped the meaning of Luigi's dissertation, he appeared quite disappointed, as if he was utterly denying its importance. But he didn't express his scepticism and merely limited himself to asking for the rest of the explanation.

'If you permit,' smiled Luigi, 'I will reconstruct only the last phase of their meanderings in Naples, just to make a point: the real suitcases, the original luggage coming to Naples by plane, were left on the Brindisi train and ended up in the beautiful port of Apulia. The pair bought in Naples on Wednesday the thirteenth had a different fate: one was driven to Rome by Marchetti and was sequestered by the police when he was arrested; the other one was disguised as Sabelli's suitcase by the tricks of the pencil-written numbers and of the name on the leather tag, and afterwards Marchetti himself took it on the Palermo train. But the clever illusion was destroyed by the blue labels on the original suitcases.'

Again, Luigi paused. Again, Boldrin showed a certain ill-disguised disappointment.

Renzi continued his train of thought in his firm, unwavering voice:

'Apart from the failure of their very clever trick, we can find a second technical mistake in their plan. Why did they leave the two original suitcases on the Brindisi train only at eight p.m., well after the other two had already left Naples: one for Rome at twenty-past six and the other for Palermo ten minutes later, at half-past six? Why such a delay in disposing of two such damning and dangerous clues as the victim's legs? Particularly since this delay also required the involvement of other accomplices, apart from Marchetti.'

Boldrin started to object, but Luigi didn't give him the time to do it:

'You could explain the delay by the absence of earlier trains, but a swift perusal of the train timetable will convince you that such an assumption would be wrong. It's a clear and obvious technical mistake by the killers, and now we arrive at their even graver, psychological, blunder. Marchetti was the only gang member known to the police, thanks to the Agliati case, so it would have been quite logical to keep him quietly out of the further, grisly development of the case. It would have been far safer if he'd tried to attract the least possible attention to himself. Instead, he tried very foolishly to be in the spotlight, in a very silly way. He gave the *wagon-lit* conductor Sabelli's suitcase with a host of explanations and recommendations. Instead of disposing swiftly and quietly of the second suitcase, he took it with him to Rome, where he was caught almost red-handed by the police. If he had wanted to be immediately suspected, he couldn't have acted in a more effective manner. A very odd demeanour for such a clever and resourceful criminal, wouldn't you say?'

Boldrin was now very confused and tried not to convey his utterly conflicting ideas:

'So, you think that....'

'I think that we must abandon the first, more seemingly logical theory that you so beautifully described, the theory of Marchetti's guilt or complicity in the crimes....'

Boldrin's common sense at last overcame his astonishment:

'But... if Marchetti didn't do it, who did?'

Luigi stopped him with a raised hand, trying to keep him calm and quiet:

'Please be patient, Boldrin. The psychological blunder made us understand that our first assumptions were wrong, and a short reflection about the two technical mistakes can put us on the right track. First and foremost, the leather tag and the numbers on the inside of the second suitcase were clever tricks to divert our suspicions, and to make us believe that it was Sabelli's suitcase—the one flown on the Dornier Do-Wal from Ostia—when instead it was one of the pair of new suitcases bought in Naples only on Wednesday the thirteenth. The reason for this trick will be very clear after my little exposition: the killers didn't have the real Sabelli's suitcase at their disposal at that moment! And the second technical mistake confirms the correctness of this affirmation, so our supposition becomes a solid fact. The real Sabelli and Marchetti suitcases were left on the Brindisi train at eight o'clock, after the other two had been sent to their fate on the Rome and Palermo trains one and a half hours earlier.'

Luigi paused to take a breath, then launched himself into the final attack:

'From the chronological exposition of the various trips of our suitcases, we can obtain a chain of logical deductions. If the killers couldn't use the two original suitcases before half past six, it means that at that very moment they were in the hands of another person, a person who wasn't their accomplice and who can only be Marchetti himself!

'So, Marchetti is certainly innocent. But we found him leaving one of the tragic, gruesome suitcases on the Palermo train, and afterwards we found him arriving in Rome with the second suitcase with Sabelli's grisly remains! If you notice that they are not the original suitcases which arrived by plane in Naples, but the new pair bought in Naples that day, you can find only one crystal-clear solution to the problem: the new pair were substituted for Marchetti's original ones. By whom? By the killers, of course! And Marchetti, needless to say, was completely ignorant of the substitution. Where did the substitution take place? In the station hall, when Marchetti was waiting for his friend.'

Luigi made the classic gesture of satisfaction of the conjuror having successfully performed a very difficult act of legerdemain. He took pleasure in explaining the trick to Boldrin in all its technical details:

'I agree with you about the first part of your splendid reconstruction: that we are fighting a very clever, resourceful and well-organized gang, having planned and effected the banker's disappearance from the plane and its terminal stop to Naples. I agree that both Marchetti and Sabelli were among its members, but I invert their positions in the gang; for me, Marchetti was the minor legman, completely ignorant of the full plan of the gang and receiving his orders from Sabelli, the only crook in the organization he actually knew. But Sabelli was scared by our investigation and by our discovery of the phone numbers on his suitcase....'

'Could we consider those numbers again, Dr. Renzi? We stopped at the first phone numbers, but... what about the other two? And the four isolated numbers? '

Luigi was slightly irritated by the interruption. Boldrin's intervention had disrupted his splendid logical explanation, reminding him of the only annoying detail he couldn't explain at all!

'Yes, yes, we shall return to it, don't worry. So, Sabelli is scared by our investigations. He knows that other members of the gang are in Naples, he knows how to contact them in case of need, he wants to warn them about the unforeseen developments in the situation....'

Renzi stopped for a moment, his rhetorical exploit waiting for a sudden thought to crystallize and solidify in a definite form, losing its momentary state of gas-like uncertain impalpability. He smiled with apparent satisfaction at the result, and he returned to reconstruct the complex machinery of the murder plot:

'Sabelli decided, with his accomplices, to book a berth for himself on the Palermo *wagon-lit*. Marchetti's presence wasn't necessary and he received the order to return to Rome. Sabelli thought to have a long meeting with the rest of the gang, so he asked Marchetti to wait for him at the station until twenty-past six, and, if he was still delayed, to leave his suitcase in the Palermo *wagon-lit*, being afterwards free to take the Rome train.'

'But that's exactly what Marchetti has been saying, word for word!'

'Why not? If he's innocent, why can't we accept his sincerity in all the details of his convoluted story? If his statement is true, it certainly can't damage our reconstruction, far from it! Now, the situation is the following—.'

Someone knocked at the door and a policeman informed the chief inspector of an emergency in his precinct:

'Someone broke into a Corso Re d'Italia office. They have found papers in disarray and a room locked from the inside, and they will force it only in your presence.'

Boldrin was quite angered by the interruption, but he looked with resignation at Luigi, feeling that his own intervention was absolutely mandatory and inescapable:

'Please come with me, Dr. Renzi,' he asked. 'It will only be a very brief pause in our discussion, and we can even continue it on the street.'

And so they did. Closing the door of the bureau, Boldrin returned at once to the subject at hand:

'So, according to you, the situation is....'

'The situation is that Marchetti is not lying and Sabelli has been killed in a trap set by his accomplices, seeing in his fear a real danger to their plan.'

'A premeditated murder? 'asked Boldrin, walking side-by-side with him on the street.

'I don't think so. Possibly he was killed by a blow in a fight, as you surmised. But they had decided to dispatch him from the moment he communicated his fear to them, following our interview. The gang had hoped that the banker's disappearance could be considered a suicide or an accident, and now Sabelli was suddenly becoming a very dangerous accomplice, ready to spill the beans to the police. So they decided to kill two birds with one stone, dispatching dangerous Sabelli in a way that could put us totally off the scent in the Agliati case. Certainly, the police would have connected the murder with the banker's disappearance, but the new danger would have been dispelled by the choice of a scapegoat, a man who could be considered guilty of both the crimes....'

'Our friend Marchetti!'

'And Giovanni Marchetti, as we know from your detective's report, was waiting for Giuseppe Sabelli in the station hall before quarter-to-five, with the two original suitcases, his own and his friend's.'

'Couldn't it have happened before quarter-to five? The two friends were released at half-past two, you know.'

'Certainly I agree that Marchetti had no alibi before quarter-to-five, and we have no solid proof that he really had gone directly to the railway station and waited in the hall for all the time. But the suitcase change wouldn't have been necessary at all, if Marchetti had been the killer's accomplice, and that's solid evidence in itself. The very fact that the murderers could stubbornly decide to execute so effectively and daringly such a risky operation demonstrates Marchetti's innocence beyond any reasonable doubt, even passing over the other evidence of the inexplicably delayed shipment of the other suitcases and of the even more inexplicable demeanour of Marchetti, far more easily explained if we believe in his innocence. The timing and logic of the plan are now strictly and solidly connected. Sabelli is ensnared in a trap and killed in a brutal fight at three o'clock. The body is sawn up and some of the grisly remains are hidden in two suitcases the gang members had previously bought, two suitcases absolutely identical to the other two they had possibly given to Giovanni Marchetti and Giuseppe Sabelli for their plane trip: the two suitcases Marchetti took to the station and that were near to him at that very moment in the station hall.

'Sabelli had spoken about him to his accomplices; possibly they were his partners in crime themselves and gave him the suggestion of sending Marchetti to the station with the suitcases, anticipating perhaps the chance of a substitution. And possibly they pushed Sabelli to book his berth on the Palermo express. At six o'clock, the murderers arrive at the station with the gruesome suitcase, one of them finds an excuse to distract Marchetti, the others easily exchange the suitcases, and Marchetti plays very gullibly and naturally the part the murderers had sneakily imposed on him. He leaves his friend's suitcase on the Palermo train, he goes to Rome with his own suitcase...and he's ready to be caught red-handed with the grisly proof of his own apparent crime. And now, with the easily explained delay, the killers have at last in their possession the real Sabelli and Marchetti's suitcases, and they can put the murdered man's legs in them and leave them on the Brindisi train.'

Luigi interrupted his reconstruction on a gesture from Boldrin. A detective was emerging from the hall of a large modern building:

'The bureau is there, on the second floor.'

On the stairs, Luigi could finally end his explanation:

'When they had the two original suitcases in their possession, at half-past six, the killers returned to the house where they had committed the crime. Certainly it was done in a closed place, out of sight of possible bystanders. They made the rest of the damning body parts disappear in the suitcases, they returned to the station and they shipped them to Brindisi on the train. And so the two original suitcases, having flown on the mysterious Dornier Do-Wal 134, could arrive as if by black magic in Brindisi with Sabelli's legs in them.'

Luigi made a gesture of satisfaction and huffed and puffed his joy to have freed himself of the wretched problem of the suitcases.

8-WHILST THE NAPLES POLICE INVESTIGATE....

On the second floor, Renzi and Boldrin found two doors. The door to the right had the brass plate of a mail-order firm selling typewriters, desks and other office material and facilities. They were promptly and ceremoniously met by the very worried managing director, a Signor Suvini, who led them along a long corridor lined with identical doors on both sides. He stopped in front of the last door on the right:

'The first person to notice something wrong was the doorman. He cleans up the offices every morning before nine o'clock, when we are still closed—.'

Boldrin interrupted him brusquely, as if he were fearing the sudden escape of a very important idea:

'So, someone let himself into the office during the night, for an unknown reason....'

Suvini stopped him with his large, raised hand:

'We're not sure, Commissario. We found traces of his intrusion in two rooms, here, and there.' He pointed first at the closed door, and then shook the handle of the big wooden door at the end of the corridor. 'You will notice that we are in the inner part of the office, the part we use as a warehouse. We very rarely come in here. Even the doorman only cleans it up occasionally. The last time was three days ago... or so he says!'

'I see.'

Boldrin shook the handle of the end door vigorously, but to no avail. 'Where is the key?'

'Here it is, the doorman found it on the floor in the other room. We tried to open the door with it, but it's bolted from the inside.'

Boldrin looked at the reddish light suffusing the sides and bottom of the door:

'The light is on. What kind of bolt is it?' he asked briskly.

'A simple iron bar fitting into a catch. The kind of old-fashioned bolt only used in country farms nowadays.'

'That's what I thought,' smiled Boldrin. 'Of course, our friends took away their own tools, but with a long-bladed paper-knife, I think....'

Suvini handed him one and Boldrin inserted it adroitly in the crack, just above the lock. Moving the blade up, he found only slight resistance, and with little effort the bar was lifted from its catch. The door swung open to reveal a sort of long cellar with a very low ceiling. The room was filled with old office desks, cases of many shapes and sizes, two unmatched chairs, a big round table in the centre and a big iron bar in a corner. A single lamp hanging from the ceiling barely illuminated the scene. Suvini was the first to enter the room, searching everywhere with his hands and his eyes and finally commenting in astonishment:

'Just like in the other room! Everything is in disarray but nothing is missing!'

Boldrin was so absorbed in his silent examination that he didn't notice when his companion sneaked out of the warehouse and directed himself towards a half-open door on the left of the corridor. Suvini tried to stop him:

'No, sorry, they entered through the other room on the right.'

'I know, I know. I just wanted to check something,' answered Luigi vaguely, going inside.

Everything was in order, of course, as he could check by looking round the room, but his attention was immediately caught by a telephone in the corner. After only a minute, he let himself be dragged by Suvini into the incriminated room on the right, but before crossing the threshold he asked the director:

'Your office hours, please.'

'From nine to three,' came the answer, without hesitation. 'After that, the work is done and we close for the day.'

Very satisfied, Renzi at last examined the disarranged office: open drawers, papers everywhere, overthrown chairs and baskets... everything was in a total, even forced and fake disorder.

'Nothing is missing?'

He knew perfectly well that the question was superfluous, and that attempted theft was not the real motive for the mysterious breaking and entering.

'Nothing. They didn't even lay a finger on the safe in my office. In any case, we don't keep vast sums of money in it, so any thief would have been disappointed.'

'If they'd really wanted to steal... but I sincerely doubt it.'

They joined the silent chief inspector in his thoughtful examination of the warehouse. Boldrin seemed quite worried:

'The motive for the intrusion seems very odd and strange. What's more, the breaking and entering was planned: they didn't force the door, they used a false key instead! I don't want to appear to be casting suspicion on your employees, Signor Suvini, but....'

Renzi let Boldrin go on for a while, but at last he stopped him, to avoid him sinking ingloriously into a quagmire of blunders and painful confessions of confusion and befuddlement:

'Please, Boldrin, come with me!'

He dragged him into the office on the left and indicated the black telephone on the wall. A white card had been stuck next to it, on which a telephone number had been written in pencil. But the chief inspector had no reaction until Renzi repeated the five numbers out loud. Only then did the sound awaken a mechanical rhythm in his memory:

'41285? But that's—.'

'Yes, the third phone number on the infamous Sabelli's suitcase! I made a mistake, only the first one was a Rome number, the 861591. A second one is here, before our own eyes, and the third one is possibly in Palermo, and refers to another base of the gang... And if you notice that this office closes at three o'clock every afternoon, or at 15.00, the last four numbers, 1519, now at last have their rightful explanation. Have you observed that many of the shipping cases in the warehouse are still full of sawdust? And that nobody has noticed that someone has stolen all the towels from the bathroom? Thus we can readily arrive at the conclusion that we have at last found where Sabelli was trapped and killed!'

When they returned to Boldrin's bureau, they found a morning newspaper on his desk, with a big headline crowned by the STOP PRESS circle:

STUNNING DEVELOPMENT IN THE FLYING BOAT
MYSTERY
VANISHING BANKER'S WIFE SHOT AT VILLA BORGHESE

Rome, night of the fifteenth

As we announced, Maria Agliati, wife of banker Francesco Agliati, who vanished mysteriously during an Ostia-Naples flight on the twelfth, arrived in Rome today from Athens with her daughter Alice Agliati. They are staying at the Hotel Flora, where they were met and interrogated by Vice Commissario Galbiati. During the evening they took a little walk in Villa Borghese, and in Corso Italia they turned left onto via del Muro Torto, almost totally deserted at that hour. They were approaching the Roman Athletic Association tennis courts when a car coming from Porta Pinciana without lights drew level with them, and four revolver shots were fired from the car.

Luckily two of them missed their targets, but Signora Agliati was shot in the shoulder and her daughter was slightly scratched in the face by a flying bullet. The tennis court night guard, Costantino Felicetti, 42, promptly came to the rescue, joined immediately by a passing motorist, Augusto Salviani, shopkeeper, who offered to drive the two unfortunate women to the hospital.

At the General Hospital, very luckily, the wounds turned out not to be serious, but both women remain in a serious state of shock. Vice Commissario Galbiati and the Squadra Volante were immediately informed of the shooting, but there are no clues at the time of writing to explain the new, enigmatic development of The Flying Boat Mystery. Nobody had noticed the car at the crowded crossroads of Porta Pinciana, and Signor Salviani barely noticed it as he was turning into via del Muro Torto from Piazza Flaminio.

As he reached the highway bridge, the mysterious car overtook him at high speed, and, finding the avenue almost entirely occupied by a cart, it jumped onto the streetcar railway low platform to the right. Signor Salviani was unable to offer any clues about the car, however, other than that it was a low, dark saloon, possibly an Alfa Romeo or a Lancia. So the new episode of The Flying Boat Mystery seems almost as inexplicable and confusing as the banker Agliati's disappearance from the Ostia-Naples sea plane. It has been reported that Vice Questore Renzi has found, in Sicily, some clues of remarkable importance for his investigation. Meanwhile, the shooting case is being investigated by his assistant, Vice Commissario Galbiati.

9-BLACKMAIL AND ATTACK

High noon. Piazza del Collegio Romano. The pavement was burning hot under the cruel July sun. In the heavy blue sky, the swallows flew away, scared by a sudden, but not uncommon, explosion of tolling bells.

Renzi met his assistant in the police headquarters hallway. Vice Commissario Galbiati was small and thin, with a certain oriental slant to his shining-black pearly eyes, always kindled with a vivacious sparkle of energetic enthusiasm.

'How are things going, Galbiati?'

'Welcome back to Rome, sir.'

They walked together, seeking the blessed shadow of the Pantheon.

'And Signora Agliati?'

'I only saw her for a few moments. She's not unwell, but she needs a few days of total rest. She's still very shaken.'

'And her daughter?'

'She doesn't know anything about the case. And as for me, I know even less than she does!'

'Splendid,' smiled Luigi sadly. 'Nothing at all about the phantom car, of course? Nothing at all about their staying at the Flora? No clues, no curious accidents?'

'According to the hotel personnel, yesterday afternoon Signora Agliati received only one phone call, from a reporter named Marietti.'

'Have you tried to find him?'

'Without result so far.'

'A false name, of course.'

'Do you think the phone call could be connected?'

'I wouldn't swear to it, but... When can I speak to Signora Agliati?'

'Tomorrow, I think, but I can't be sure about it!'

They arrived at the famous restaurant La Rosetta, highly cherished by Luigi, and he invited his assistant to lunch. Galbiati was so obsessed with his sense of duty that he tried ceremoniously to resist, but Luigi managed to drag him into the pleasantly fresh, dark old rooms where the deserted white-clothed tables gave a slight feeling of neglected isolation, soon dispelled by the excellent *spaghetti alla carbonara.*

'This morning I had only a coffee and a brioche,' explained Luigi.

Galbiati enjoyed his chief's momentary silence, then asked him what he had discovered in Naples.

'Everything and nothing, my dear Galbiati. Marchetti is certainly off the hook. I know how, why, where and when Sabelli was killed but I don't know who did it, so....' He gave a semi-comic sigh and ate silently for a long and mournful moment. 'Getting back to Rome, my dear Galbiati, what about the crew?'

'As you asked, I contacted SANA and they—.'

'Excellent, Galbiati.'

Luigi reflected for a moment, whilst the waiter disappeared with the empty dishes:

'All that's left is our disappearing banker. You've requested his luggage from Brindisi, but it hasn't yet arrived in Naples. I fervently hope it will not be as full of surprises as the other four! Remind me whether he arrived with it at his Rome hotel.'

Galbiati sighed:

'Yes, and he asked that it be sent via the Hotel D'Azeglio van to Termini Station. It was a very bulky luggage, I hope you don't think.....'

'My dear Galbiati, I have heard Commissario Boldrin doing a lot of plausible reasoning about a return ticket to Brindisi.'

'A return ticket to Brindisi?'

'Agliati's ticket. It was in his briefcase, but where do you keep a railway ticket, when you're travelling? In your pocket, of course, or in your pocketbook. So I'm beginning to have many doubts about Agliati's trip....'

Galbiati smiled, not all that convinced. He liked Renzi, he was a good man and a friendly boss, and he admired his mind and his clever, unconventional methods, but he talked too much to be a good policeman. For Superintendent Galbiati, policemen had to act first and talk later, and then only if required. So he was relieved when his chief returned to a more business-like conversation:

'Have you discovered anything else about his stay in Rome? How did he get to Ostia, that morning?'

'We found a cab driver named Giovanni Pratesi, living at 14, via

Ancona. On the morning of the twelfth, at eleven o'clock, he picked up a passenger for the Ostia sea airport from Piazza Venezia. He remembered him very well because he was in a great hurry and they argued about the fare. I didn't have Agliati's picture, so his identification is not certain, but he did describe him as a fat, tubby middle-aged man.'

'And, of course, he was in a hurry because he had been delayed and didn't want to risk missing the plane. Well done, Galbiati. The description is quite good, and certainly Signora Agliati will have her husband's picture for better identification. She's Greek, isn't she?'

'Yes, but Agliati, as you know, was Italian by birth and took Greek citizenship only fifteen years ago. They were married in 1918.'

Renzi looked thoughtful:

'He was in Athens for a year whilst he was founding the Italy & Greece Bank... But have one of these splendid Burbank Californian prunes, my dear Galbiati!'

He offered him a big, juicy violet prune, but Galbiati refused politely.

'An apricot, then?'

'No, thank you very much, sir.'

'Don't stand on ceremony, Galbiati. Pick a Burbank, do me a favour!'

Galbiati accepted reluctantly and returned to business with a shadow of a smile:

'Agliati went to Greece from Milan in 1917, with a regular Italian passport.'

Renzi smiled with pleasure. He was having both a prune and an apricot. But he sighed and turned to another question:

'What was his business in Italy, before Greece?'

'So far, nobody knows. But I hope to receive more information from Milan, this evening or tomorrow morning.'

They talked lazily for some time, because they were reluctant to return outside under the cruel, white-hot Roman sun. The white-clothed table in the quiet, cool, dark corner was far more inviting. They smoked a bit in silence and only when the hands reached three o'clock did they find the courage to go outside.

'My dear Galbiati, I shall return home for an hour. Is Signora Agliati still in hospital?'

'No, she returned to the Flora this morning.'

'Please pay her a visit and try to obtain a recent photo of Agliati, then try to find our cab driver again. I'll phone if we can take him to HQ for questioning. Sorry, I must leave now, here's my bus!'

Pratesi, the small, alert cab driver, answered Renzi's questions promptly. But Agliati's picture gave him his first moment of perplexity:

'Yes, he was middle-aged, grizzled, and quite fat, but I don't remember him having a moustache... and he seemed darker and younger.'

'And he didn't have a moustache?'

'I didn't study him closely, but I think I would have remembered if he'd had one... And he seemed balder, too!'

Renzi had a sudden thought. He selected some snapshots from a drawer and handed them to the witness:

'Do you recognise any of these?'

Pratesi picked out a snapshot, and, peeking over his boss's shoulder, Galbiati recognised the bank teller Larini!

'That's him, for sure! He looked just like that when he refused to give me a tip.' Pratesi was once again assertive. Renzi and Galbiati exchanged disappointed looks, then released the driver. Galbiati compared the two snapshots:

'They do look vaguely similar, yes.'

'So now we know less than before. We'll meet again this evening.'

Renzi made a very depressed exit and tried to put some order in his very muddled thoughts with a little walk under the fierce Roman sun. But it was too fierce, and when he turned onto the boulevard he wisely decided to take a bus to his next destination: Piazza Colonna and the Metropolitan Bank.

After a short ride, he was in its offices, semi-deserted because it was almost five o'clock. He recognized the stocky Larini amongst the tellers and asked to speak to the director. He was absent, so Renzi was obliged to question the head of personnel, Deputy Director Santini, a middle-aged, undistinguished, bald-headed man, with pale and motionless eyes and face, and very expressive and movable thin lips, the only distinctive features in his vague and anonymous countenance.

'Yes, certainly we sent Larini to Palermo. The Direttori and I decided on it together. It was a very urgent business deal. Our Palermo branch is working on a merger with the Corleone Bank, and Larini had to take the plane to Palermo that very morning: he was taking confidential papers of the utmost importance, vital to closing the deal. Regrettably, the forced stop in Naples and consequent delay hampered operations, and the deal was not as beneficial to us as it would have been the day before.... '

He began an extensive explanation of his bank's losses, numbers to hand, but Renzi thanked him and excused himself, only to face the white-hot Roman sun yet again. Santini was warmly and deeply in love with the sound of his own voice, but for some reason Luigi didn't share his affection.

At 44, via Condotti, in the offices of the Italy & Argentina Bank, he found a very different atmosphere. The clerks were a bit too fawning in their attentions, and Managing Director Marsigli weighed his words carefully. He was tall and dark, with finely-chiselled features, an alert eye, and the glib words of the clever fox, finding a smooth way out of every tangled situation.

Luigi attacked him with his usual sharp alertness:

'You have very strange clerks, Commendatore Marsigli.'

'I beg your pardon?' Marsigli looked attentively at him.

'Your bank sent a notorious ex-convict to Tunis.'

'To Tunis? To my friend and correspondent, the director of the Simoun?'

Luigi was irked by the cautious answer:

'Yes, you sent him confidential papers using a man called Pagelli, an old jailbird involved with illegal emigration... An old friend of the police, not your usual common or garden variety confidential messenger!'

Marsigli's grey eyes lit up with an angry sparkle:

'Just a moment, please.' Through the intercom he ordered Assistant Managing Director Sandri to be sent to him immediately. Renzi had been longing for such an interview. Sandri's phone number was the first one noted casually by poor Sabelli on his suitcase. The man was tall and skeletal, with steel-rimmed spectacles, trousers that were too short, and high buttoned boots. Marsigli introduced him to Renzi:

'Dr. Renzi is warning us that the Bertieri fellow we sent to Tunis with my letter to Morangis is an ex-convict named Pagelli!'

Sandri showed the requisite astonishment:

'An ex-convict?'

Renzi, irritated by the show of incredulity, clarified:

'An ex-convict, jailed for aiding and abetting illegal emigration to America.'

'Did you know about this, Sandri?'

'Not exactly, sir,' babbled the befuddled assistant managing director. 'I mean to say, certainly not! I was informed that Bertieri was not a model employee, but they told me only that he had been a daredevil youngster, doing the usual silly things youngsters are always doing... but nothing more, and now he seemed on the right track, very anxious to earn his money honestly. A good worker, eager and efficient in his work....'

Luigi interrupted the usual long list of ready-to-use compliments:

'Who recommended him?'

'Our man in Viterbo, if I remember rightly,' replied Marsigli, comforted by Sandri's prompt nod.

'We didn't have anyone else on hand and he seemed very good for the job. My letter to Morangis was merely technical in nature, and he did splendid work in Tunis, in any case,' concluded Marsigli smugly, dismissing Renzi with a look of annoyed disinterest about the whole question.

So Luigi skipped any allusions to Giuseppe Sabelli and was gently escorted out by Sandri. They exchanged some vague courtesies and Renzi asked him bluntly:

'What do you think about the Metropolitan Bank? Is it quite solid?'

'I very much hope so: it's owned by our group,' Sandri replied, with the ghost of a smile on his mournful countenance as he led Luigi through the bank's monumental doorway.

On July the sixteenth nothing happened. Signora Agliati was doing better, but Renzi had to wait another day to question her. Nothing emerged about Sabelli and Marchetti; nobody knew how they had spent their time before the deadly trip to Naples. The press was at last informed about the mysterious and grisly suitcases, and Renzi couldn't stop them from tying Sabelli's murder to The Flying Boat Mystery.

The Milan police had found no traces of a Francesco Agliati having left Italy for Greece in 1917. The mystery was growing darker and more muddled, but Renzi was not worried: the affair was so tangled and complex that a single clue could instantly solve it... if only it could be found!

The following morning, Signora Maria Agliati was sitting in her suite at the Flora. She was a natural blonde, and her quiet blue eyes and rosy, fresh face masked her real age of forty. She was still pale, but she was calm and in full control. Her daughter Alice, a gracious girl of fourteen, swiftly vanished from the room. Luigi enquired politely about Signora Agliati's health, refraining from assuming an official tone, so the interview had more the appearance of a social visit. It was Renzi's way of conducting an investigation, and certainly neither Galbiati nor Boldrin would have approved of it. But social sensibility doesn't preclude insisting on the tactless subject of her husband and his mysterious past, and even more mysterious present and future. Maria had met him in Athens in January of 1918, when he had founded the Italy & Greece Bank, but he had never told her the motive for his emigration to Greece:

'He was very vague, he hinted only at some business problem. He had suffered heavy losses for his partner's misdeeds... But he never told me any details, and I never knew what kind of business it was!'

'So these heavy losses determined his decision to leave Italy for good?'

'I don't know, maybe they happened some years before. Really, he was quite vague about it!'

Luigi was very thoughtful and he murmured almost to himself:

'Of course, or in 1917 he wouldn't have had the capital to found his bank, immediately after his arrival in Athens.' He lifted his head in his habitual resolute gesture as he moved to the decisive question:

'And yesterday ? Nothing happened before....'

A shadow darkened the quiet blue eyes for a brief moment. But was it a shadow of incertitude, or did it mark a painful recollection?

'Nothing at all,' she answered uncertainly.

Renzi waited again before asking about the phone call she had received at the hotel, and his patience was fully rewarded, perhaps because Signora Agliati had guessed the nature of his next question:

'You will understand, Dr. Renzi, that I would much prefer to not speak about a certain circumstance... but yesterday a reporter named Marietti phoned me at the hotel at around four o'clock.'

'Did you know him?'

'Not at all, but he told me that it was for a very urgent and important question....'

'Signora Agliati? Marietti of Il Popolo di Roma. I beg you not to speak to anybody about... Signora Agliati?'

'Speaking.'

'I'm Giuseppe for this conversation.'

'But—.'

'It's about your husband, Signora Agliati. I have in my possession, I can't tell you how, certain papers about him that, if they were to be published, could....'

'I forbid you to do so.'

'They are about his business before leaving Italy, you know... Do you understand?'

'I understand only too well, and I know that Francesco had nothing to reproach himself for, they were his business partner's—.'

But the communication was suddenly interrupted. Signora Maria Agliati was speaking into the void, and in some ways its emptiness scared her more....

Luigi listened to Signora Agliati's tale in total silence, and made no comment afterwards. He excused himself for having reminded her of the unpleasantness, and tried to calm the now very agitated banker's wife down. When she had become more or less herself, he made his gallant exit from her suite.

In Piazza Collegio Romano, at police HQ, he spoke very briefly with Superintendent Galbiati and asked him to call the Milan police and to request urgently all possible information about the most important business affairs happening between January and September 1917. But Renzi also added certain details which rendered their task far easier and swifter and, ultimately, successful.

10-LOVE AND SHOPPING

After Termini Imerese station, Vallesi entered the compartment where Marcella was sitting alone. He gave her a shy greeting, but she limited herself to a nod. She was too tired to express her desire for solitude.

She was just too exhausted to make any sense of her very muddled feelings. She was tired, terribly so, and terribly sad. The trip to Palermo had dispelled all her previous hopes....

She tried to forget the young man seated in front of her, but his anxiety ended by exasperating her, and at his very first words she couldn't restrain herself:

'Miss Arteni, I must—.'

'You must just leave. At once!'

Marcella was even irritated by her irritation. So she tried to justify her excessive outburst of anger:

'You and your policeman friend.'

'My policeman friend left on the two o'clock express.'

'So why didn't you go with him? '

Giorgio looked at her in silence, then he whispered, in a clear tone which he hoped would be persuasive and penetrating:

'My friend had guessed the reason for your trip to Palermo.'

Marcella remembered Renzi on the deck of the ferry-boat. He was quiet and solemn, but spoke in a friendly voice when he had told her with a smile: "The friends of our friends are our friends, Signorina Arteni! " And maybe he hadn't been so wrong after all.

'But he didn't tell me anything, and when you disappeared in Palermo without a word, after our arrival, I didn't know how to find you, so I permitted myself....'

Marcella wondered why she let him talk so much. His words were dulled and darkened by a sort of grey mist, possibly created by her own lassitude. But at least she'd had the time to rearrange her feelings, and irritation and anger and tired apathy no longer occupied the first steps of her emotional staircase. Another memory sneaked insidiously into her mind, almost unnoticed at first: another train running in the dark, and she and Vallesi, with the same silence uniting them in the darkening solitude of a compartment in the growing dusk.

Their first kiss was witnessed by the curtains of rain veiling the Gulf of Salerno. And Capri, where so many love stories are born in so many romantic novels, hid itself, mysterious and prudent, behind its veil of mist.

For the tenth time, Giorgio anxiously awaited the arrival of the car in front of the terminal in Piazza Flaminio. For the tenth time he searched eagerly, and at last Marcella descended from the tenth Inner Circular Car.

'Thank you for coming, my dear Marcella!'

'You didn't believe I would, did you?' smiled Signorina Arteni teasingly.

Giorgio answered with a look of joyful admiration and mock reproach.

'In any case, I can't give you too much of my time today, Giorgio. That is, if you don't want to be my courteous Cavalier in a very long and boring shopping trip.'

'Your Cavalier is at your willing and obliging service, my lady! Actually, long and boring shopping trips are my specialty. Satisfaction guaranteed.'

They headed towards the Ponte Margherita, and Marcella told him with cautious amusement about her trip home.

Renzi had guessed correctly, the Arteni household was not a happy one. In the last few years, the marriage of Marcella's parents had deteriorated, beginning with the not-too-improbable suspicions of the very jealous Gianna Arteni. But, as often happens, it was her husband's own singular suspicion which caused the break. If they had been quiet and understanding people, they would have quickly been able to work out a solution. Instead, in the last three years Gianna Arteni had been running around Europe with a merry group of friends, whilst Marcella had remained in Rome with her father.

Recently, based on her father's words and her mother's letters Marcella had glimpsed the possibility of a happier future. She had discovered that her mother would be stopping in Palermo on July

12th, and decided to take the chance of obtaining from her a first expression of regret, from which so many others might flow. She had no time to lose, however, and caught the plane before her father could prevent her. But after she had been forced to stop in Naples, her father had caught up with her, and she had been obliged to confess to him the reason for her flight. She had escaped again, however, and found her mother on Pellegrino Mountain. But her mother had no regrets at all and failed to pronounce the desired words. Despite that, her father seemed to Marcella to be far more affectionate and happy than in the past. Marcella fervently hoped it was a good omen.

Her tale ended with a smile as they arrived in Piazza Cola di Rienzo:

'And now for my shopping! The most important thing is a box of ping-pong balls!'

'Do you play ping-pong?' asked Vallesi with a smile.

'And tennis, too! I'm an ace, you know!'

'And with whom do you play?' asked Giorgio.

'I will confess only after a whole hour of hard shopping,' laughed the girl, dragging him along via Lucrezio Caro.

The Sisters Adamoli's shop was a long, dark and narrow room almost completely filled with the colourful rubber animals that are the joy of baby swimmers. Two young boys were pushing their mother to buy a splendid yellow and blue duck with an enormous twisted neck. Marcella gaily rummaged through the rubber monster menagerie and she returned to Vallesi with a very long green and yellow crocodile.

'Would you like this, as my present to you?' She happily twisted it around Giorgio as a monstrous rubber belt and stood back to admire the startling result:

'In a few years, you'll have a big paunch like that and you won't be as good-looking and lovable, my dear!'

She put the crocodile back and selected a box of ping-pong balls instead. As she was about to leave, she noticed that Giorgio had picked up the crocodile again.

'Really, if you want it that much....'

But Giorgio wasn't hearing her puzzled words, he was hearing Luigi talking about Agliati's paunch. And just suppose the paunch had been false and made of rubber...?

And so he arrived at a very odd solution to the impossible Flying Boat Mystery....

Giorgio was a bit uneasy meeting Renzi, because he'd been back in Rome for twenty-four hours and hadn't had time for even a very brief phone call. But his friend welcomed him cheerily:
'Love can excuse and pardon everything.'
'Listen, Luigi, I've discovered... everything!'
And he narrated the visit to the via Lucrezio Caro shop, Marcella's joke and his thoughts about Agliati's paunch... The word had a magical effect on Renzi:
'Heavens, you could be right.' But he was very cautious, trying to not to get too excited by his friend's theory. 'That would mean he's been wearing a false rubber paunch for ages!'
'Why not? As a disguise, when he left Italy suddenly in 1917!'
'Ridiculous! A false rubber paunch can't modify your look that much, and it certainly wouldn't render you unrecognisable! A pair of false whiskers would be a far better disguise!'
But Vallesi wasn't convinced and he tried to argue from a different angle with even greater energy:
'Perhaps he disguised himself only when he arrived in Ostia. Nobody on the plane knew him....'
'Nobody knew him,' repeated Renzi, in an oddly impassionate way.
Their demeanour reflected their very different temperaments. Giorgio walked nervously around the room with his fists jammed into the pockets of his jacket as if he wanted to measure it from wall to wall; Luigi, on the other hand, was deeply ensconced in his armchair as though he were freezing in that hot summer afternoon , barely moving his head from left to right as he mechanically followed his friend's erratic wanderings. He was trying to reorder his own ideas after that alarm bell. They had found a small break in the case, and he was trying to enlarge its size. He was used to letting people talk and talk, whilst he, by contrast, was refining his own ideas. Renzi was a good talker, but an even better listener.
'So, you think that the solution—.'
'Of course, Luigi, of course! I've disposed totally and completely of every impossibility! And it's the only way it could have been done, believe me. If Agliati passed through the skylight....'

'Just a moment, please. 32 centimetres by 39, let me see....'

He cut out a paper rectangle of the same dimensions, pressed it against the window, and asked quietly:

'Good. And then?'

Vallesi looked at him in embarrassed astonishment.

'And then?' repeated the assistant commissioner. 'Where is the body? If only we could find it!!! Even if we accept your solution, the easier explanation, the accident, is still absolutely impossible. The skylight is on the roof of a very small toilet, and, in order to fall from it, Agliati must first have pushed his body through it. He couldn't have done it accidentally, that would be ridiculous!'

'Yes, if he took off the false paunch, he could plan an escape, or a suicide!'

'No, suicide is also impossible. I can admit that, in sudden panic, Agliati could envisage—.'

Vallesi rushed to interrupt him, inspired by a sudden thought:

'Of course, of course! Wonderful, perfect! On the plane, Agliati was very worried. He feared he had been followed, and suspected several of the passengers: the ex-convict, and his travel companions Sabelli and Marchetti. So, when I announced that there was a clandestine passenger in the cockpit, he became very fearful—.'

'Allow me to speak, please! I admit that he may have been worried about the presence of a mysterious clandestine passenger, and I can admit that he could have lost his mind and wanted to commit suicide. If he had been at a fourth-floor window of a building, possibly he might have thrown himself from it, but from that skylight? No, it's too ridiculous, he would never have contemplated such a bizarre and impractical suicide method. He would never have conceived such a complicated and difficult way of killing himself, even if he was inspired by a sudden fear... No, he found the opening too narrow, even if he removed his false paunch... and in the meantime the fear would have subsided and he would have tried to escape instead of killing himself!'

'So, he escaped!'

'Yes, he decided to escape, to disappear!'

Renzi thought for a moment about this last theory: a deliberate disappearance! He had hinted at this very plausible solution to Boldrin when he had explained the points of the case to him, with a certain egotistic rhetorical self-conceit. But his inborn pragmatism pushed him to more simple and realistic problems:

'Yes, but how could he escape? He couldn't have had a parachute, it's not so easy to hide as a false paunch, is it?'

Vallesi seemed lost in thought:

'Couldn't he have found an easier way out through the luggage compartment? From the hatch on the roof....'

'And if he had fallen during his daring escape?'

'His fall would have been seen by the other passengers, from their windows. And you've already stated that the body hasn't been found!'

'That's not so important. Even if the body had fallen near to the coast, because sea planes usually follow the land during their flight, it could easily take nine or ten days before it was found.'

'But someone would have seen him fall from their window! The passenger cabin is behind the toilet, nearer to the tail. If Agliati's fall was accidental....'

'An accident following a deliberate and very odd escape,' commented Renzi quietly.

'Yes, but an accident is in some ways a natural cause, independent of human planning. So, how do you explain the murderous attack on Signora Agliati and her daughter?'

'You have a point, and it's not the only inexplicable circumstance.' Renzi seemed quite shaken. 'So, do you suspect murder, and not an accident independent of human planning?'

He had let his friend talk in order to clarify his own ideas, but now, under the spotlight, Giorgio's theory was becoming more plausible, far beyond Luigi's expectations. But it wouldn't be the first time a reporter had solved a case before the police... Gaining confidence, Vallesi elaborated on his idea:

'For me, Agliati was escaping, and he feared someone on board, so his first impulse was to hide and then run away. If he had been thinking about killing himself, as you correctly said, he changed his mind at the first obstacle he encountered. But his fear and desire to escape his foes did not change. He removed the false paunch in order to escape through the skylight, the only possible way out. As he was crawling along the fuselage, the paunch fell down into the sea. He directed himself towards the only other opening, the hatch of the luggage compartment, easy to open even from the outside. He assumed the compartment's wooden door would hide him from the other passengers... So he opened the hatch and found himself in the compartment with the mechanic!'

'The mechanic?' repeated Luigi in astonishment.

'A very corrupt one, as we know only too well. So Agliati could easily bribe him from his well-padded wallet. Franceschi was easily persuaded to help the banker escape.... '

'And suppose he murdered Agliati for his well-padded wallet?'

The reporter reflected for a moment:

'And threw the body from the hatch? In order to steal the banker's money?'

'Yes... and possibly for another reason,' murmured Luigi, possibly just to provoke his friend to see his reactions.

'I really don't think that Franceschi murdered Agliati in cold blood. He certainly couldn't have anticipated that the banker would escape through the toilet by removing a false rubber paunch and crawling along the roof so as to get into the luggage compartment! Of course, he could have killed on a sudden impulse out of sheer greed and thrown the body into the sea through the hatch, even if it is odd that nobody heard their fight, or that no clue could be found in the compartment. But, after the plane landed, both the mechanic and the plane were fully searched and nobody found the money or the rings or the watch of the murdered banker! And I really don't think that Franceschi could be a sadist, killing bankers purely for pleasure!'

'And so?'

'And so, I remember very well the mechanic first coming out of his lair in the luggage compartment, just a few minutes after Agliati went into the toilet. No, really, I don't think he had the time to kill him and throw away the body! Ah, I'm beginning to see!'

'What?'

Giorgio was very pleased with himself:

'Everything! Franceschi took a parcel from the cockpit!'

'I know.'

'And what did it contain?'

'Some bread and some fruit, his usual lunch.'

Vallesi had a self-satisfied smile:

'No, I'll tell you what it contained: a mechanic's overalls!'

Luigi was really surprised:

'A mechanic's overalls? What do you mean?'

'I'm pretty sure my deductions up to this point are correct, but it still remains to be explained how Agliati could escape from the plane after it landed. The mechanic was his accomplice, but he certainly couldn't have stolen one of the pilots' parachutes from the cockpit. So Francesco Agliati was obliged to wait until the landing in Naples. And he found the right moment, the right opportunity, to disappear: even though everyone's attention was focused on the breaking down of the door and the activity around the toilet, someone would have noticed a passenger climbing out through the luggage compartment hatch. And, since the wharf was under strict surveillance, there would have been nowhere to go. But nobody would have noticed a mechanic leaving the luggage compartment in his customary blue overalls. Who would ever have thought to stop him for questioning?'

This classic rhetorical question ended his explanation. Giorgio was very pleased with himself.

Luigi reflected in silence on the theory, pushing his critical mind to try to find any possible hole in it.

'So, you think that the banker is still alive?'

'Of course!'

'So how do you explain the attempted murder of his wife?'

'I admit I haven't really tried to explain it,' smiled Vallesi. 'Certainly, Agliati had enemies, as his escape proves. Perhaps his foes wanted to kill his wife as well.'

'I could understand it if they'd tried to kidnap her, but to kill her....'

And at that very moment, Renzi had a sudden intuition of the truth. It was a mistake to consider the attempted murder as an isolated, self-contained incident. No, it was strictly tied to the attempted blackmail of some hours before, and this connection could explain both acts very easily. It's highly unusual for a blackmailer to attempt to kill the person he is trying to blackmail; he would prefer to scare her into accepting his conditions. But the mysterious assailant had certainly tried to murder her, and certainly he was the same person who had tried to blackmail her before. He was menacing her to reveal her husband's past. That would explain the logic of the murderous attack: the killer didn't have any revelations to make, instead he feared the revelations she could make! The phone call was a shot in the dark, to ascertain what she knew about her husband's Italian past. Her protests had scared her husband's foes, and they had decided to strike immediately.

But what value could the wife's words have? Her reaction had been only a very understandable, indignant protest, apparently... Could such very vague words really have pushed the mysterious criminals to attempt a very dangerous and daring attack in a Rome street?

Luigi was lost in thought and had completely forgotten his friend. He vaguely heard Giorgio in the nearby room, on the telephone. The first words he understood were certainly part of a phone call to Signorina Arteni... But Vallesi returned almost immediately to announce to his friend:

'Goodbye, I'm going to Naples!'

Luigi looked at him lazily:

'Have a nice trip, and please return with the banker, dead or alive!'

11-RENZI'S WALK

After Vallesi had left, Luigi immediately phoned Chief Inspector Boldrin, then put on his hat and took a walk in the Rome streets, where the first lights were announcing the approaching dusk. He allowed himself to be dragged half-consciously by the crowds towards Piazza Colonna. Normally he very much liked Rome at that hour, and liked to watch the faces of the unknown passers-by, with the cautious and curious diffidence of an art critic at the personal showing of a new artist.

But that evening he preferred the quieter and darker streets around Fontana di Trevi to Piazza Colonna and the animated via Tritone: via dei Crociferi, via dei Lucchesi, via dell'Umiltà, via della Pilotta, Piazza della Pilotta....

Renzi let himself be guided by the regular rhythm of his steps. His mind was a tangle of fragments of words, splinters of theories, brief sparks of luminous and uncertain ideas, all tied together, and all sharply and neatly separated in a glorious confusion, like the pearls of a torn necklace he was desperately trying to reconstruct, random puzzle pieces of an abstract, indescribable mosaic.

He let himself be absorbed by the mood: a flying boat in the air for ninety minutes from Ostia to Naples, with sixteen people on board at departure and only fifteen on landing....

In his mind, he reconstructed the diagram of the inside of the plane, placing each actor at the appropriate spot. Larini and the pilots in the cockpit. Larini... his sudden departure, his anxiety to be on board the Dornier Do-Wal 134 could be suspicious, but his director Santini's explanations had apparently let him off the hook. Certainly, Larini had never left the cockpit. Could Vallesi have been right when he asserted that Agliati's fear was caused by a clandestine passenger, even though he couldn't have seen anything of him through the glass doors: not his face, nor even his shadow?

But Vallesi had also thought that the cause of Agliati's fear could have been Pagelli, the ex-convict... Luigi thought that hypothesis far more plausible, even though the ex-convict, just like Larini, was travelling on the Dornier Do-Wal 134 for a perfectly valid business reason. Larini was actually even more suspect, because he had wanted to be on board that particular plane! Perhaps Larini's guilt seemed less plausible only because Pagelli was an ex-convict, and thus a far more shady character....

Two other shady actors in the drama were Sabelli and Marchetti, particularly since their grisly Naples adventure could perhaps be tied in some way to the banker's disappearance. When he remembered those suspicious characters: the ex-convict, the clandestine teller, and the so-called corn tradesmen, Renzi had the odd feeling that their very presence on board the plane could have created a dark and menacing atmosphere of fear, murder and betrayal. Were they all partners in that menace? Were they all accomplices? Renzi would really have to reconstruct how the menacing atmosphere could have led to a mysterious murder on the Dornier Do-Wal 134.

These melodramatic rhetorical questions surprised even Luigi himself, but his ironic smile reflected the reality of the situation: he just didn't know how the presence of those four strange passengers on board was darkly connected to the banker's disappearance. A situation enhanced by contrast, if he remembered the other passengers in the cabin.

The lady in red, consumed by her rebellious act, fearing yet hoping to hear her husband's footsteps behind her....

Marcella Arteni, perhaps not thinking too much about her sudden flight in quest of her mother, not daring even to hope for a highly unlikely reconciliation of her parents, and trying desperately to distract herself by following the route on the airline token map, looking at the landscape out of the window, and perhaps—why not? —looking surreptitiously at Giorgio....

Giorgio, thinking and looking only at her, but absorbing semi-consciously the disturbing, menacing atmosphere all the same....

Maria Martelli, possibly experiencing some doubts and fears about her expedition, but greedily attracted by the coveted stocks and shares waiting for her in Palermo, after an expensive and dubious trip decided after so much hesitation....

Her husband, following her in silence, not daring even to think....

Those were the actors in the passenger cabin.

Behind the wooden door, in the luggage compartment, the

mechanic, so suspect according to Vallesi's theory. Possibly an accomplice, or even a dark leading villain of the piece. But Luigi had immediately noticed a tiny detail which completely demolished his friend's case. He had phoned Naples to verify it, and Boldrin had confirmed his doubts, but he was still waiting for the definitive confirmation. But if Giorgio's theory was destroyed, how then to explain the leading actor's movements; how to explain Francesco Agliati's vanishing act? Why extract the banker so easily from the toilet through the now comfortable skylight, only to leave him afterwards, lost and desperate on the flying boat's fuselage, without a direction to take, a goal to reach?

Luigi tried another approach: he methodically laid out a chronological reconstruction of the various actors' movements on stage before the shocking climax of the piece, the first announcement of Agliati's possible disappearance.

TIMETABLE
1. Sabelli goes to the toilet and comes out almost immediately.

2. Vallesi goes to the cockpit and returns, announcing the presence of a clandestine passenger.

3. Agliati goes to the toilet, where he locks himself in and vanishes.

4. Franceschi, the mechanic, goes into the cockpit and returns to the luggage compartment with a parcel.

5. Marchetti tries to go to the toilet and finds the door locked. He knocks and, receiving no answer, gives the alarm.

With these five points firmly established in his mind, Renzi decided to leave the dark and quiet streets around Trevi and head for the Prati Borough. He was tired and would have preferred to expunge everything about The Flying Boat Mystery from his thoughts, but in his half-asleep state the disparate, clashing elements of the case were continuously whirling in his mind, and continued to do so even whilst he was in bed. They continued all through the dreamless night and into the busy morning after....

'Telephone, Dr. Renzi. A call from Naples.'

Luigi had hoped to speak with Boldrin, but instead it was Giorgio:

'I'm calling you because I've possibly found a trace... A man looking very much like our friend took a cab near to the port at about one o'clock, that same day.'

'How do you know?'

'Sheer chance, a lucky strike, if you like. I found the driver, and he picked up a passenger no more than two-hundred metres from Beverello Wharf. The man wore an overcoat and was completely muffled in a scarf and felt hat. In July, under the Naples sun, just imagine!'

Luigi answered in an impassive, emotionless tone. It was his poker voice, one might say:

'Where was he headed?'

'Mergellina Station, where I am now. A ticket clerk seems to remember a fellow buying a first-class ticket to Rome, a few minutes after one o'clock. He remembers being surprised because it was a slow-moving train, used only by locals....'

'That's quite a coup. Did he have any luggage with him?'

'I didn't ask, but I can if you want. I'm on my way to Rome now.'

'I thought that might happen!'

'Let me speak, please. I'm on my way to Rome, but I won't arrive until four o'clock. I have two hours to wait before my train, so I called you so you could start making enquiries in Rome.'

Renzi's poker voice didn't change:

'Very good. See you later, then!'

Five minutes later, he received another call from Naples. It was Chief Inspector Boldrin at last. After a very brief conversation, Luigi looked at his watch: it was half-past ten, and he could reach the Flora Hotel in a twenty-minute walk. By eleven o'clock he could, very conveniently, be received by Signora Agliati.

He waited for a quarter of an hour in the foyer, but scarcely paid attention to the slow motion of the hands on his watch. He frowned as he thought of his fruitless chase after the elusive fragments of the case. He permitted himself the ghost of a smile as he imagined his friend in Naples, in a cloak-and-dagger pursuit of cab-drivers, ticket clerks and muffled murderers in overcoats.

The arrival of the slender Signora Agliati shook him out of his reverie.

'I'm sorry to disturb you again, but—.'

The woman waved away his apologies. Luigi looked in silence at her smooth, serene face. She didn't seem overly hungry for news of her disappearing husband. Possibly she was too young and beautiful for a fiftyish banker.

'Do you have any news about....? Have you found him? '

'Just a few more clues, and I have something more to ask....'

She made a gesture of surprised acceptance.

'Do you really not know why your husband left Italy for Greece? Nor what his business was before founding the Italy & Greece Bank? When he suffered those heavy losses you told me about yesterday?'

'I've answered your question, and it's the only answer I can give you, Dr. Renzi....'

He moved his chair closer to her armchair:

'Really, I wouldn't insist, if it weren't strictly necessary...Your husband's disappearance is directly linked to the attack on you, I'm afraid, and it seems probable that the explanation for both crimes could lie in your husband's past.'

'I understand that perfectly well, but I can't tell you what I don't know,' she replied with the shadow of a smile.

'The attack on you and your daughter was both logically and chronologically preceded by the phony reporter's call, a call quite possibly instigated by the same criminals who organised and executed your husband's disappearance. They tried to blackmail you about your husband's activities in Italy before his emigration to Greece, and it's easy to surmise that the criminal gang we are fighting was formed and headed by a person or persons linked to your husband's Italian past, possibly even the same business partners who caused the heavy losses your husband suffered.'

In the young woman's eyes Renzi could read only a quiet and patient, almost indifferent waiting. Slightly irked by it, he continued his questioning more forcefully:

'I'm at a loss to understand how the few words you uttered in response to the phony reporter could have motivated such a daring and risky attack on you. How they could be so frightened by your very vague negative answer. You can readily understand the importance of any possible detail you may have neglected to tell me. If you could only suggest a name to whom we could direct our investigations....'

But Renzi realised at once that his efforts were in vain. If the answer could be really found in Agliati's past, he would have to wait for news from the Milan police.

At half-past four on the afternoon of Tuesday, July 19th, eight days after Francesco Agliati's disappearance, Giorgio Vallesi arrived in the Rome Termini Station from Naples.

He phoned Marcella to invite her to dinner that evening and then rushed to police HQ. Unfortunately Renzi wasn't there, having visited his office at about three o'clock, solely for the purpose of taking a police car to Ostia. Vallesi was quite surprised and wondered whether his friend was questioning the two pilots and the mechanic again. But he had to contain himself, with Marcella's help, until he managed to reach Luigi by phone, later that evening.

His friend arranged for him to be accompanied by two detectives the following morning, during a long, tiring and utterly futile series of enquiries at Termini Station. Meanwhile, Renzi stayed home, to read with great attention the dossier on Agliati, which had just arrived from Milan.

At a few minutes past noon, Vallesi made a visit to Piazza Collegio Romano. In the absence of Renzi, he was received by Superintendent Galbiati, who asked him with a malicious smile on his impassionate, official face:

'Have you read *Il Messaggero*?'

'I didn't have time.'

'Of course, due to your inquiries at Termini Station... I suggest you read it now.' Another mysterious smile. 'It's very interesting. The reporter attaches great importance to the false rubber paunch and to the possibility of a deliberate disappearance.' Noticing Vallesi's worried surprise, he again put on his air of official seriousness. 'Don't fret yourself, it was only a joke, he never thought to consider such a fantastic hypothesis!'

The headlines blared:

THE FLYING BOAT MYSTERY.
AFTER A WEEK OF INVESTIGATIONS,
WHAT ARE THE POLICE DOING?
OUR SOLUTION TO THE MYSTERY

Rome, July 20th.

Banker Francesco Agliati disappeared more than a week ago, and after a week of unsuccessful investigations, we can only ask what the police are doing to throw some light on this dark, obscure mystery.

We are ready to admit that they took resolute action when they promptly arrested Giovanni Marchetti for the murder of Giuseppe Sabelli, another passenger of the unlucky Dornier Do-Wal 134. But they had very damning and concrete evidence against him, and his arrest could not in any way help the other investigation, The Sabelli Murder Case being a completely separate criminal episode, having no connection whatsoever with Agliati's disappearance. Nor could it be of any help in the investigation into the notorious attempted murder of Signora Agliati, a crime executed very possibly by a gang of blackmailers trying to exploit Signora Agliati's difficult and uneasy position after her husband's disappearance.

The same gang, headed by a phony reporter calling himself Marietti, had tried to blackmail the poor woman, and was very likely responsible for the attack on her in via del Muro Torto afterwards. Signora Agliati had shown strength by promptly rejecting the blackmail threat, and the thugs very probably thought they could scare her, thus demonstrating a total disdain for a possible investigation, fully consistent with a daring and well-organized criminal gang.

We can inform the public about its existence, without any possible fear of hampering the other investigation, because our theory is shared by the police and we know that they have taken all possible measures for unmasking them and blocking any attempt to escape justice. But, unfortunately, the first and most important mystery remains without solution.

Our readers will remember that we presented from the very first day the only possible, clear, patently simple solution: Francesco Agliati had committed suicide. Now we shall again demonstrate that it is the *only true solution of The Flying Boat Mystery. As the mathematicians say, we shall proceed ad absurdum. If it was not a suicide, it must have been an accident or a murder. Murder is materially impossible. There is no trace whatsoever of a deadly trap set in the small toilet before Agliati's arrival, and when he did enter he locked himself in, thus excluding any possible contact with anybody on board. Nobody went into the toilet after him, as all witnesses have confirmed, and as demonstrated by the intact lock and bolt still blocking the door when it was broken down. An accident is equally impossible, as the only egress from the toilet is a skylight in the roof which nobody could reach accidentally, but would be very comfortable for a person contemplating suicide.*

Vallesi tore his eyes angrily from the printed page. Why had Galbiati asked him to read this rubbish which added nothing new to the mystery?

'Why are you wasting your time reading this stupid string of platitudes?'

Galbiati looked at him with his customary official gravity:

'Superior orders... Dr.Renzi thought it was the best material they have written about the case, and he must have had his reasons.' Once again, his forced gravity seemed to contain a tiny speck of irony. Once again, there was the ghost of a smile: 'I can't do otherwise than share his opinion with you.'

Vallesi was beginning to suspect his leg was being pulled, and didn't know whether to be angry or to answer one silly joke with another.

Luckily the phone rang and spared him a decision. Galbiati answered, and commented to Vallesi afterwards:

'That was Dr. Renzi himself. He asked me about your plans for the afternoon.'

'I don't know, as yet. I hope to be very occupied this evening....'

Again Galbiati had a very curious smile:

'Of course,' he gravely sympathized.

'And in the afternoon I wanted to return to the station, even if it seems that the phantom passenger who came that Tuesday from Naples.... '

'Another mysterious disappearance, I see.' Galbiati's sphinx-like smile was becoming utterly unnerving. 'Dr. Renzi would be very pleased if you could be here, in the bureau, at about six o'clock. If you really can't make it, you can always phone, but it would be better if you could come personally. You can also invite Signorina Arteni, if you should happen to meet her.'

'Signorina... do you mean Marcella?'

'I believe that is her name, yes. Dr. Renzi suggests that it would be appropriate if she would wear an overcoat, and be wrapped and muffled. A drive in an open car in the evening can be awfully refreshing, even in this season.'

'In an open car?'

Vallesi was not very original with his questions when he was surprised.

'An Alfa Romeo, I presume.' Galbiati was clearly, albeit unofficially, amused by the reporter's dumbstruck expression. He continued cordially: 'Permit me to point out that you did not give proper attention to the brilliant example of journalism I had offered for your not-so-patient perusal. Possibly you didn't read the last few lines.'

He proceeded to deliver a stentorian reading of the article in question, revealing unexpected dramatic skills:

"Our suicide solution seems to have at last convinced even our police. Dr.Luigi Renzi has happily decided to abandon the farfetched and utterly fantastic theories he was toying with last week, finally accepting to see the problem in the light we had shed on it. The proof he has surrendered to our mathematical reasoning can be found in the information we have just received from a reliable source: today at dawn, Naples and Rome police have organized a full search by sea and by land, along the coastline from Ostia to Naples, for Francesco Agliati's dead body."

'Vice Commissario Galbiati, sometimes you really astonish me!'

12-RENZI'S ACTIONS

Giorgio phoned at six o'clock, and again he was only able to speak to Superintendent Galbiati:

'Dr.Renzi was here until half an hour ago, but he was obliged to go out again. He begs you and Signorina Arteni to kindly meet him in Piazza dei Re Di Roma, if you know where that is.'

'Piazza dei Re Di Roma?'

Vallesi was reverting to his mindless echo.

'Out of Porta San Giovanni, on the Appia Nuova. Dr.Renzi is waiting for you in front of Number Three.'

Once out of the Porta San Giovanni, the taxicab drove for a few minutes on the crowded highway, then stopped in Piazza dei Re Di Roma. Giorgio and Marcella found themselves in a wide circular space surrounded by a tall wall of buildings, with a ring of streets around two small parks traversed by streetcar rails and the straight Appia Antica. They looked at the house numbers, trying to orient themselves, and below the rightmost wall of the tall and almost identical buildings they noticed a big Alfa Roadster in front of Number Three. Renzi was at the wheel and introduced the other three passengers. Amongst them Vallesi was astonished to recognise the high commissioner himself:

'Commendatore Bertini, Brigadiere Sagni, Brigadiere Pinardi....'

Commendatore Bertini bowed gallantly towards Marcella, and helped to settle her in the car by his side, while Vallesi was vainly and peevishly questioning his friend about their expedition. For half an hour, the general conversation was represented only by Bertini's courteous attempts to entertain Signorina Arteni, and by Renzi's vague answers to the persistent questioning of Vallesi, doing his best impersonation of an investigative reporter.

Suddenly there came a powerful rumble from the Appia Antica, and a large motorbike stopped alongside the Alfa. Seeing the high commissioner, the officer lifted his dusty goggles and gave a military salute:

'All right?' asked Luigi.

'All right.'
'On the Casilina?'
'On the Casilina.'
'And Giorgi?'
'I left him at Porta Maggiore, he's following them.'
Luigi made a swift calculation:
'They have ten minutes on us now... A Lancia Dilambda, if I'm not mistaken. How many people in it?'
'Three, including the driver.'
Luigi looked at his five companions, including Signorina Arteni. But the high commissioner encouraged him with a nod:
'Don't worry, the others will give us a hand. But we should leave immediately, they have a good start on us!'
'No problem, I will overtake them before Frosinone.'
Renzi noticed a slim girl entering Number Three, and executed a brilliant racing start in her honour.
Via Appia, Piazza Santa Croce, Porta Maggiore... with the thumb constantly on the horn, Renzi raced madly through the crowded streets, leaving a wave of angry protests in his wake.
They jumped and jolted on the rough suburban surface, before an inviting, seductively smooth asphalt ribbon helped them in their efforts. The Alfa ate up the kilometres without ever letting the speedometer drop below 120.
The descending twilight obliged them to slow a little on the Valmontone slopes, but once night had truly fallen, the brilliant artificial light of the Alfa pushed her swiftly towards the alluring lights of Ferentino.
On the wide turning road descending towards the plain after Ferentino, another motorbike appeared in the luminous square painted by the Alfa's lights. The high commissioner touched Renzi's shoulder. He gave an understanding nod and approached the bike at the next turn. He signalled with his lights to the mobile officer, who kept alongside the car. The high commissioner shouted from the car:
'Everything all right?'
'All right, sir.'
'Where is the Dilambda?'
The officer pointed at the dark plain where the wide turns were dimly visible in the night. A white caterpillar of light crept towards

the sparkling, distant hill of Frosinone.
'Anything to report after Rome?'
'Nothing, sir.'
Renzi turned towards his chief:
'If you think, sir....'
'As you wish.'
Pinardi passed his notebook and pencil to the high commissioner. Bertini swiftly wrote down some words and gave the paper to the bike officer:
'You know what to do. Pass along these orders at once.'
'To Naples and Pozzuoli,' added Luigi, his foot itching on the accelerator.
'Yes, to Naples and Pozzuoli,' echoed his chief.
The bike officer saluted Bertini as the car continued its mad dash along the road. The bike light flashed for a moment behind the Alfa, then disappeared into the night, far, far away, whilst the roadster began to eat up the road behind the creeping white caterpillar. Renzi hurtled towards Frosinone and at last, when they entered the town on the top of the hill, his lights could pick out the clear shape of a powerful speeding car. Bertini touched Renzi's shoulder again, inviting him to rein in his battle horse. The driver obeyed promptly, but not before commenting with satisfaction on the accuracy of his calculations:
'We caught up with them in Frosinone, as I predicted.' He looked at the car clock. 'Even if they are quite speedy themselves, we've covered eighty kilometres in fifty minutes, including the brief slow down... An average speed of 95, not so bad!'
Renzi was going at a very slow pace now, keeping his distance from the escaping car. Entering Frosinone, he had switched the lights to low beam, keeping them there even when they were out of town. In so doing, he was rendering the chase more difficult, but if he were to keep the escaping car in his sights, he couldn't risk revealing himself by a too powerful, long and indiscriminate beam.
The chase continued through the darkness, splintered by the Dilambda's lights into a thousand fantastic, ever-changing shapes, in a whizzing and whirring kaleidoscope of running arabesques. But swiftly the night closed in as a silent accomplice of the pursuers.
After Frosinone, Ceprano, Cassino, and Caianello....

Now, after two and half hours from the start, the two cars, still separated by only a few hundred meters, traversed the bridge across the Volturno River and entered Capua. The escaping car slowed briefly in hesitation, then swiftly turned to the right, leaving the main road.

Renzi stopped next to a sign at the crossroads. One arrow pointed straight ahead to Naples and indicated a distance of ten km. The arrow pointing to the right indicated instead that they were at one and a half km from Giugliano and sixteen from Pozzuoli.

Renzi activated the dashboard light and he and Bertini perused a road map of Naples area in its dim glow. Renzi pointed to an intersection only a few km to the south of Aversa:

'We're here, you see, with Pozzuoli on the right. For five kms the road goes straight, posing no problem, but after Qualiano there is a fork....'

'I see,' replied Bertini. 'With the road to Pozzuoli on the left, and a small road down to the sea on the right.'

'To the sea and to Fusaro Lake and Baia.'

Renzi followed the red line of the road with his finger, to a point before Procida, after the blue oval of Fusaro Lake.

Bertini nodded and reflected for a moment:

'Possibly they will choose that road, in order to stay away from big towns. But we could pick the other road, which is longer, but safer and quicker. So we could stop at Pozzuoli and be able to check whether everything is going according to our predictions.'

Renzi drove quickly towards the small village of Giugliano. He slowed briefly in Qualiano where their route crossed the Terracina road, and, as they had foreseen, he could still see at the distant fork the red lights of the Dilambda, turning right towards the sea.

After ten minutes he stopped at the Pozzuoli police station, ran inside, and was soon back in the car:

'Everything is OK.'

He continued rapidly along the road framing the gulf between Pozzuoli and Baia. After the small town, he left the main road and the coast and proceeded in the inner countryside until they met a road coming from the right. He stopped and examined the fork, using the moving searchlight of the car:

'Have they been here?' shouted the high commissioner from the

Alfa.

'I have found clear tracks of Michelin tyres, the kind used on the Lancia Dilambda,' replied Luigi, returning to the driver's seat.

'Proceed, but with caution,' ordered the high commissioner.

They proceeded very slowly along the country road, passing a level crossing and the fork to the right for Torragaveta, and found themselves in a deserted hollow. After a few hundred metres of turtle-like, cautious exploration of the countryside, Luigi stopped the lights and the car. He took a few steps in the dark and pointed at the shape of the Dilambda, barely visible in the soft embrace of the night.

As they cautiously approached the car, a shadow detached itself from the dark bushes on the roadside and gave a reassuring military salute to his chiefs. The officer pointed at the empty Lancia:

'You can proceed safely, all three men are gone!'

'Where are they?'

'Behind that thicket on the left.'

'How did you get here?'

'By bike from Naples.' He pointed to a tangle of handlebars and wheels, hidden in the shadows behind the bushes.

'OK. Lead us to them!'

They reached the thicket by a small path on the left. Behind every bush was a motionless shadow, watching. Their guide stopped and beckoned to Luigi with a silent gesture. They knelt down and peered through the darkness, hidden behind the tangle of brambles and twigs. Behind them, Bertini, Vallesi and Marcella approached with cautious curiosity. To the right, beyond the thicket and the side of the hollow, lay a half-barren meadow of withered, sparse grass, in the middle of which, darkened by the vivid blue of the summer night sky, could be seen the shape of a big man seated or crouched on an oblong rock. But was it a man, or a voluminous crate?

At the end of the barren meadow, they could see two more shadows, moving about as if they were trying to orient themselves or find some lost object. Possibly they were searching for a place, without remembering exactly where it was.

After Luigi spotted the two new actors of the mysterious drama, he exchanged a few words with Bertini, then whispered to Vallesi:

'Please stay here with Marcella. I don't think they'll offer any resistance, but it's better to be safe.'

Giorgio understood that the amazing night drama was approaching its denouement. Renzi was observing the stage from the bushy wings, as the master director. Now there were three shadows circling the odd shape in the middle, and Giorgio could see that it was definitely a very big crate.

Luigi raised his arm. Eight, ten, twelve men emerged from the trees and bushes and circled the three shadows around the box on the oblong rock:

'Hands up!'

The three shadows were so stunned by the sudden circling assault of this army of darkness that they immediately surrendered, without any attempt at resistance. Renzi and the high commissioner broke the circle of darkness with the beams of their powerful torchlights. Bertini gallantly left the centre stage to his young assistant and master detective. Renzi approached the three captives and directed the beam of his torchlight to the big box on the rock:

'There is the dead body of Francesco Agliati, the banker murdered eight days ago, and there is his murderer!'

He lifted the beam to illuminate the tall figure of Commendatore Marsigli, managing director of the Italy & Argentina Bank.

13-RENZI'S EXPLANATION

Four people were seated at a corner table in the Miramare Restaurant in Pozzuoli. They were High Commissioner Bertini, Giorgio Vallesi, Marcella Arteni and Luigi Renzi. Three of them had confined themselves to coffee and pastries, but Luigi had before him an almost empty dish of noodles with mussels, and a waiting steak drowned in a forest of green salad. Vallesi used any possible space between two fork-loads of noodles to try to interview his friend:

'But how could you suspect Marsigli? When did you solve the mystery of the banker's disappearance?'

'I'm very sorry, I wasn't watching the clock at that historic moment! But I wouldn't ever have solved the case without your smiling friend's help.'

'You really are a gentleman,' said Marcella, 'but I don't know how.'

'Please, don't deny your indisputable contribution! That's why, with the kind permission of Commendatore Bertini, I invited you to the exciting dessert of this mysterious affair. I broke some rules in doing so, but really you deserved it! Nobody would ever have solved The Flying Boat Mystery without the timely rubber paunch of my friend Giorgio; your gift suddenly provided me with all the required answers.'

Marcella answered with a kind nod, but now she was smiling at Giorgio, and Giorgio alone. Renzi continued with mock and hilarious humility:

'Heavens, I can't deny having had some suspicions even before my return to Rome. During our investigations in Naples I was immediately puzzled by the return ticket in the banker's briefcase... why wouldn't he have carried it in his pocket, or in his wallet? And the notorious phone numbers in Sabelli's suitcase... Everything made me suspect the presence of hostile enemies of Francesco Agliati. And there were too many banks involved: the Metropolitan Bank rushed Larini to Palermo, forcing him to be on board the Dornier Do-Wal 134 in a very suspicious way, whilst the Italy & Argentina Bank was doubly compromised by the assistant manager's phone number in Sabelli's suitcase, and by the mysterious trip to Tunis of Bertieri-Pagelli. But the rubber paunch trick, if it could explain the escape from the toilet, restored the same degree of probability to all four options for Agliati's disappearance.'

Vallesi proceeded to list them, once again:

'Accident, suicide, murder and purposeful escape.'

'And the clues didn't necessarily point to murder. I refer to the clues I had noticed before the suspects' release, because after their release the killers made their first mistake. Our adversaries committed three grave errors of psychology, errors that ultimately gave us a great advantage in our clash of minds. Only the third mistake was deliberately and knowingly suggested by us; the first one was committed even before we could decide any possible course of action, and the second involved a field of investigation completely different from our actual line of enquiry. So, for two of them, we can't claim any credit at all. Think about it: what happened to Sabelli and Marchetti when they were released?'

'Sabelli was murdered....'

'Exactly. And that was their first mistake; a mistake caused by an excessive belief in our powers of deduction, and by an excessive fear of the very few, miserable clues in our possession. Both Sabelli and Marchetti were members of the criminal organization responsible for the banker's disappearance, but they certainly weren't its leaders; Sabelli was simply Marchetti's contact, the mouthpiece transmitting his bosses' orders to him. Marchetti was a very low-level accomplice, completely ignorant of the other members' names, plans and goals, so they could easily leave him in our hands without any fear for their own safety. Neither Sabelli nor Marchetti had any knowledge of Agliati's fate, they simply received the order to be on board that particular plane, and we shall talk later about the necessity of their presence there. So, you can easily understand their amazement and fear when they found themselves involved in a very dangerous police investigation. Sabelli had more to lose, and his terror was very obvious when we discovered the numbers marked on his suitcase and we could correctly understand the real meaning of the first group....'

'But what did the other numbers mean?'

'One was the phone number of the office where Sabelli was trapped and killed. I haven't as yet found the meaning of the other, but very possibly it was the phone number of a Palermo den of the gang. Sabelli had rushed to note the numbers on his suitcase when they gave them to him by phone, so he could use them in case of emergency. The emergency presented itself with our Naples investigation. When Sabelli was released, he immediately phoned the local den of the gang. We identified and arrested the Naples members of the gang, who were successfully organizing, together with their Roman accomplices, headed and covered by the Italy and Argentina Bank, an extensive ring of clandestine emigration smugglers. Witness the highly competent participation in it of our old friend Pagelli.

'So, Sabelli informed his accomplices about the current, dangerous situation, and they were amazed and terrified by the unforeseen development of the police investigation, and by Sabelli's arrogance: certainly, he was trying to find some personal advantage in the present quandary. His partners in crime invited him into the den to discuss the new situation and they ordered him to send Marchetti to the station with the suitcases. Marchetti also received the order to wait in the hall for his partner until twenty-past six ,when he was due to leave for Rome, having previously left his friend's suitcase on the Palermo train, in the compartment he had just booked.

'Sabelli then goes to the office in Corso Re d'Italia, where he has his appointment with death. Please, try to enter into his accomplices' minds while they wait for him: his phone call has shown the total collapse of their optimistic plan. Not only did the police not immediately buy the suicide-accident hypothesis they tried to sell, but they also discovered and correctly interpreted the phone number of one of Italy & Argentina Bank's top managers. Furthermore, good old Pagelli, who was travelling on the Do-Wal 134 on behalf of the same bank, was immediately recognised by Commissario Boldrin as an ex-convict. So they understand that they must completely change their tactics. And Sabelli has intervened to create new complications, with his arrogant demands of the gang. The useful minor accomplice is now very dangerous, with his threats and blackmailing demands. They originally intend just to kidnap him, but he fights back with unsuspected energy, and the violent quarrel becomes a violent murder.

'So, the killers now have a completely new problem to solve: they must hide any clues to the murder, and dispel any suspicion about

Sabelli's murder and Agliati's disappearance. It's obviously no easy task, but they have on hand a very good scapegoat, ready for use: Giovanni Marchetti waiting with his suitcases in the hall of the railway station. With daring swiftness they execute the plan they have just devised. They buy two identical suitcases, fill them with Sabelli's grisly remains, exchange them with those of Sabelli and Marchetti, and wait confidently for Marchetti to put one of them on the Palermo train and take the other with him to Rome, ready to be caught red-handed by the police. They fill the other two suitcases with what remains of poor Sabelli and leave them on the Brindisi train.

Signorina Arteni asked shyly:

'But you had already determined that Marchetti was innocent.... '

'Without informing the public, needless to say! The killers tried too hard to force Marchetti's apparent guilt on us. They made some minor mistakes, and these tiny details were very revealing if you weren't dazzled by the too-flashy clues the murderers had put under our noses, fearing that we wouldn't notice them. But the first tiny chinks showed immediately that their armour was made of cardboard and paste. The killers' deft move had the opposite result and they ended up caught in their own clever trap. Marchetti wasn't accused of Sabelli's murder or Agliati's disappearance and the failure of the trick demonstrated clearly their own involvement both in the murder and in the disappearance. They had been eager to show a connection in order to accuse Marchetti of both crimes, but in doing so they were actually revealing their own hidden game, rendering their own position more and more dangerous and unsafe. Connecting the murder to the disappearance gave to Agliati's vanishing act a far more tragic and definite meaning, with the result that, amongst all the plausible options, only one became the obvious real solution: murder! '

'It was murder, of course,' exploded Vallesi, 'but how was it done? And why? Marsigli wasn't even on the plane!'

Luigi put down his hard-working fork and raised his hand to calm his friend:

'That was the situation after my Sicilian trip, where I could at least narrow the field, scratching off many unjustified suspicions and far-fetched hypotheses. Before my return to Rome, my dear Giorgio, I really couldn't have answered your questions. I had only a vague idea about the culprits, but it seemed quite clear that the Italy & Argentina

Bank was the evil spider in the centre of the deadly web. But two very different events permitted me to solve the other mysteries, thus discovering the killer's motive and method. The first event chronologically was a consequence of the second grave mistake, the attempted murder of Signora Agliati. The second event happened purely by chance: Marcella's joke in the Adamoli Sisters' shop in via Lucrezio Caro.'

Vallesi smiled at Marcella, and instantly his eyes softened in warm intimacy, whilst he remembered with tenderness their first wanderings in the Rome streets, after the dark shop and its rubber menagerie.

'The attempted killing of Signora Agliati was a disaster, a catastrophic move dictated by a grave error in psychology. The first mistake was the preceding phone call: the phony blackmail threat was instead a clumsy trick for trying to discover if the banker's widow knew anything about her husband's past in Italy before 1917. The widow's answer was unwittingly ambiguous and they began to think, quite wrongly, that she did in fact know everything about her husband's past.

'So, they decided to kill a very dangerous witness before she could set the police on the right track, and that was the motive for the via del Muro Torto shooting. That attempted murder was a grave mistake, and it gave us almost immediately several clues about the real reason behind Agliati's disappearance. We suddenly understood that we had to investigate what Agliati had been doing in Italy before leaving for Greece in October 1917. Certainly, "Francesco Agliati" was an alias he assumed when he left Italy for good. The banker was apparently from Milan, but the Milan police couldn't find any trace of a Francesco Agliati before his emigration to Greece. Widening our field of investigation, we asked the Milan police for news about every big business deal before October 1917. The other morning, whilst working my way through the files they supplied, I came across Antonio Marsigli's name. He had been involved in a major case of war profiteering, and immediately the strong suspicions I had about him (he had sent Pagelli to Tunis; his assistant manager's phone number was in Sabelli's suitcase; his bank controlled the Metropolitan Bank, who had so mysteriously sent Larini on that very plane to Palermo) suddenly became a rock-solid certitude.'

'But why did he hate Agliati so much? Why did he commit all those murders?' asked Marcella.

Luigi smiled at her:

'To answer your question, I will begin, as in the best fairy tales, with "Once Upon a Time." Once upon a time, there were three big, bad wolves, named Antonio, Francesco and Giovanni. They became very, very rich by selling sub-standard goods to our Army during the war: cardboard shoes for our soldiers; woollen uniforms being woollen in name only; poor or spoiled food for their mess. Everything was going swimmingly for them, until they decided to cheat each other, despite the fact that their profiteering in that sad age before the big Caporetto defeat, when Italy really risked being invaded by Austria, was making them as rich as any crooked Croesus of this cruel and dark world. They could have continued to share their ill-gotten gains quietly and happily, but instead Giovanni and Antonio decided to enhance their shares by denouncing Francesco to Italian justice. Of course, Francesco had no intention of paying his toll alone, but the others had powerful political friends who hushed up the scandal on their behalf. But poor Francesco could at least enjoy the offer of a new, clean, tailor-made passport, and the imperative advice to leave Italy for good in the next twenty-four hours with a good padding of big, green notes. It's hardly necessary to tell you that the name on the new passport was Francesco Agliati. But along with the green notes, very unfortunately for the others, our Francesco thought to take with him some highly compromising papers and receipts, rendering his dearest friends' sleep not so quiet and peaceful.

'These papers certified some unsavoury contact with the enemy and could have ruined the lives of a long list of political bigwigs. Although Francesco couldn't use them during the war, the politicians being too powerful at that time, he just had to wait for the right political moment, with his ready-to-use papers always near to his greedy, vengeful hand. When the war ended, Giovanni decided to end his own miserable life as well. That left Antonio to face Francesco's revenge alone. In the meantime, of course, both adversaries invested their loot wisely: Francesco became Francesco Agliati, CEO, owner and founder of thriving Italy & Greece Bank, and Antonio became Commendatore Antonio Marsigli, top manager of Italy & Argentina Bank Group. Of course, Antonio knew only too well who Agliati was, and, fearing more and more the papers in his possession, he began a fierce secret financial war, almost terminally wasting Francesco and his bank. Then he contacted his ex-partner in crime, proposing a gentleman's agreement which was in reality a deadly trap. Thus did he entice the wary Signor Agliati to Rome, where the trap worked perfectly, and he was killed right on schedule, as Marsigli had planned.'

'In Rome?!'

Both Renzi and Bertini smiled at Vallesi's amazement:

'Yes, my dear Giorgio, in Rome. And now I will answer your last question: how was it done? It was the most important, artistic and difficult part of the whole plan. I admit that for a long time I was completely in the dark, how could the banker have vanished into thin air from that small alcove on the flying boat? For a fat man like Agliati it was completely and utterly impossible! But the rubber toys in the dark menagerie in via Lucrezio Caro provided the solution for me, and ultimately a rubber crocodile cracked the case with its rubber jaws. It was a very promising discovery, but, as we quickly discovered, all it did was to send us back to square one, with the four options having the same, equal, identical degree of possibility. Had Agliati escaped, had he been murdered, had he killed himself by his own hand or had he died in an unfortunate accident?

'For many practical considerations, the accident was swiftly discarded as a plausible option: the body was not seen in its deadly fall by any of the passengers, it had not been found on the coast, even if the plane had followed it in its route, and an accidental death couldn't explain Sabelli's murder and the attack on Maria Agliati. We discarded suicide as well for the same considerations, even without pointing out the ridiculous absurdity of the means Agliati was supposed to have chosen for killing himself!

'We also discarded murder, because it would have been a random, senseless, meaningless crime, very difficult, if not impossible to execute. The murderer could only have been Franceschi the mechanic, the only person who had the opportunity to see the banker after his daring escape from the toilet, but Franceschi had no apparent motive for Agliati's murder. Furthermore, the body had not been found, and it would have been quite impossible for Franceschi to make it disappear from the luggage compartment.

'Even Vallesi's theory about Agliati's wilful escape, a very promising and interesting hypothesis, had to be discarded. It was a plausible mechanism, but it was too complex, too difficult to be executed with the necessary precision. The proverbial grain of sand would have immediately stopped that infernal clockwork machinery. But it was not a grain of sand which blocked and terminally damaged Giorgio's very clever clockwork theory. It was a peach nut, a simple peach nut. Vallesi's theory was that Agliati had escaped from the plane in Naples from the luggage compartment hatch, disguised in the mechanic's overalls which Franceschi had taken into the cockpit in the famous parcel the passengers had seen under his arm. A very simple and effective disguise, yes, but the mechanic had affirmed that the parcel contained only his lunch, a lunch made of bread and fruit, or more precisely of bread and peaches. When I phoned Boldrin he confirmed to me that in his very thorough search of the plane he had indeed found peach nuts in the luggage compartment, which had certainly not been present at the departure from Ostia. And I had separate confirmation myself from the Ostia airport cleaning crew.'

'But these nuts....'

'Don't think too much about them; Franceschi had some juicy peaches for lunch, and that was it. In any case, Agliati would have had to have been very lucky to escape unscathed and unobserved from a wharf completely surrounded by wary, eagle-eyed policemen! And his escape would render completely inexplicable and senseless both Sabelli's murder and Maria Agliati's shooting. And, of course, the very presence of Agliati's dead body in the crate Marsigli had transported in his Lancia Dilambda from Rome to Pozzuoli scratches your theory off our list of possible options.'

The high commissioner had smiled at the destructive energy of his assistant against poor Vallesi's theory, but now he decided to deflect the other's impetuous assault with a prudent diversion:

'But by discarding all four options, you end up in a blind alley with no possible way out, exactly like poor Agliati in his toilet, my dear Renzi!'

'Actually, I confess that, for a moment, I thought that the rubber paunch discovery had dragged us from a blind alley into a blinder one. Agliati could have got out of the toilet, but afterwards where would he have gone? Passing through the skylight onto the plane's fuselage, he could only go to the luggage compartment, through the hatch on the roof. And after that? I tried to reconstruct the actors' movements on stage and the variations that happened on board after his vanishing act, with this simple diagram. Permit me to show it to you....

	MOVEMENTS DIAGRAM	A	B	C	D	
1	Situation on departure	3	0	12	1	16
2	Agliati goes to the toilet	3	1	11	1	16
3	Possibly Agliati escapes to luggage	3	0	11	2	16
4	Situation on arrival	3	0	11	1	15

A is cockpit; B is toilet; C is passenger cabin; D is luggage compartment.

'From this diagram, it's easy to understand that, not including the possibility of Agliati's presence in the luggage compartment after his visit to the toilet, the only person to have been alone and unseen in a part of the plane, completely out of the passengers' control behind a wooden door, was Franceschi the mechanic. And this diagram allowed me to solve The Great Flying Boat Mystery, *the flying boat that Francesco Agliati was never in!*'

Luigi watched Marcella and Giorgio's faces with enormous pleasure and self-satisfaction. Vallesi could barely splutter out:

'But... but... but we all saw Agliati on board the plane!'

'You only saw Franceschi the mechanic,' replied Renzi quietly.

'Franceschi... the mechanic? '

'I think that it would be best to begin again from the beginning. Marsigli had enticed Agliati to Rome—Agliati with his damning papers. We don't have a lot of precise details about Agliati's visit, but I think I can reconstruct it accurately enough using my peerless imagination. Marsigli welcomed Agliati, trying to allay his suspicions. They had a couple of meetings, and in the second one, early that Tuesday morning, Agliati was promised a fat check by way of payment for the dangerous documents in his possession. Possibly the original meeting was planned to be in Naples, as the return ticket to Brindisi found in Agliati's briefcase, where it had slipped due to a grave error by the killer, suggests. But they moved the meeting to Rome, because the greater distance to the airport offered Marsigli more possibilities for his clever plan. Of course, Agliati never had any intention to go to Naples by plane, he simply wanted to return to Brindisi quietly by train. So, Marsigli promises Agliati a fat check and he lures him into a trap. He drives him in the Dilambda to the D'Azeglio Hotel, where the banker must collect the shipment receipt for his luggage; after this last precaution, Agliati will be completely in his foe's hands. In the Dilambda, Marsigli drives him to his mansion outside the Porta Cavalleggeri. In a secluded corner of the park there, we have just found traces of the recently dug pit where the body was hidden before its last trip to Pozzuoli.'

'But... the mechanic?' asked the impatient reporter.

'He was at the Ostia airport, waiting for his accomplices. They took him the various elements of his disguise: the rubber false paunch; the glasses; the suit; the banker's briefcase. He was also awaiting another actor of our little play, Larini the teller, who was to be rushed very urgently to Palermo by Santini, the Metropolitan Bank's Vice Commendatore, acting of course under Marsigli's orders. Please don't forget that the Metropolitan Bank is owned and controlled by the Italy & Argentina Bank Group.'

'But if Agliati was dead, why did they want Larini on board the plane, why....'

'I'm very sorry to say that with your silly question you are demonstrating that you haven't understood a whit of their so-clever plan,' replied Luigi peevishly. 'Larini's presence on the Dornier Do-Wal 134 was mandatory, absolutely necessary. They couldn't have done it without him on board. Just as it was absolutely necessary that Pagelli, Sabelli and Marchetti be on board, too. The deadly trio of phony country tradesmen were called to occupy the last available seats, so that a last moment passenger like gullible and reliable Larini couldn't find a place on the plane. Larini was sent to Palermo at the very last moment with strict orders to be absolutely in Sicily that evening at any price, so they knew very well that he would have used every possible trick to get aboard the only available plane. Of course, Franceschi, the oh-so helpful mechanic, was ready to present himself and to apparently accept the bribe he was in reality forcing the other to offer. And so Larini would travel in the cockpit with the pilots, and Franceschi would be secluded in the only invisible and uncontrolled part of the plane. There, alone, invisible and uncontrolled by anybody, he could swiftly change his own appearance and happily play his double role in the flying boat drama. But now it was actually only a comedy, the real drama having happened before, far away, in

Marsigli's mansion outside Porta Cavalleggeri, where he had coldbloodedly killed his ex-associate and blackmailer, the only true and authentic Francesco Agliati.'

'But when did the mechanic become the banker?'

'These are the facts in strict chronological order: a few minutes before take-off, Franceschi is seen by everybody, in his mechanic's overalls, talking to Larini, thus creating a perfect alibi for himself. The passengers are led to believe that he will be secluded in the luggage compartment, where he will quietly remain on his own until they see him exiting from it an hour later. But he doesn't go into the luggage compartment, he doesn't even board the plane then. Instead, he goes into the adjacent empty hangar where his accomplices have surreptitiously brought the banker's disguise in a limousine. With a good rubber padding and Agliati's glasses, suit and briefcase, he perfectly looks the part. So, in a jiffy, the humble mechanic can become the powerful banker. Nobody on the plane knows the real Francesco Agliati, so he can rush on stage, ready to seat himself in Agliati's reserved place, delivered by limousine behind the remains of the crowd around the plane. So, our little diagram is absolutely and totally wrong: the twelve seats are all occupied, but nobody is in the luggage compartment. You can imagine the phony banker's disquiet when Giorgio reveals to everybody that Larini and the mechanic have traded places. And what if somebody, for instance Giorgio, the professional nosey-parker, should go into the luggage compartment for a peek? So he decides to accelerate the plan and rush into action. He locks and bolts himself in the toilet; he discards out to sea the false paunch and the rest of his clever disguise; he climbs onto the fuselage through the skylight, closes it, and goes on a little walk along the fuselage to the luggage compartment hatch, an easy task for a mechanic, used to acrobatic emergency repairs during the flight; the hatch is easy to open from the outside, he descends through it into the luggage compartment, and he's ready to dress in his usual overalls and to go into the passenger's cabin for another little comedy act. He takes his lunch in the cockpit, he returns to his closed compartment and quietly awaits the shocking ending , eating, to my great envy, bread and juicy peaches. '

Luigi peeled a second orange with an ill-concealed pleasure. It was a red orange, his favourite kind. In a religious silence, under the patient eyes of his public, he made the bloody slices disappear, whilst the others used the pause to try and rearrange their very confused thoughts. As usual, Vallesi was the mouthpiece of their doubts and of their collective amazement:

'But this evening... why are we here? Why did we come to Pozzuoli? And the crate, the car chase, the dead body... what's the meaning of all this madcap nightmare of an adventure? How could you foresee that....'

The assistant commissioner looked with great satisfaction at the remains of his feast on the white-clothed table. He was about to answer his friend, but this time he was preceded by Bertini:

'Our friend Renzi was convinced within a few days of Marsigli's guilt, and had fully understood the stunning flying boat trick, but he had no real, concrete evidence. The flying boat trick was a total failure, because it missed its real objective: to deceive us about the real scene of the crime, and redirect our investigations to a place where the dead banker had never been, pushing us to ask ourselves vainly and ineffectively how and why he had vanished, when his disappearance had happened far before the take-off in a completely different place. But even this failure of a trick could guarantee the culprits' safety, because, by changing the time, the circumstances and the scene of the crime, it successfully hampered our investigation of the real disappearance. The Sabelli Murder Case and the shooting of Maria Agliati provided no clues at all, because neither the notorious phone numbers on Sabelli's suitcase nor Agliati's and Marsigli's crooked escapades during the war could constitute real evidence against the banker's killers. So we had to act, to push our opponents with a daring move to make a very false step, forcing them to unmask themselves by their own hand. And that was their third mistake, a mistake suggested and forced on them by our friend Renzi with a very skilful trick. Your friend stole your thunder, dear Vallesi, and he himself wrote that silly article in *Il Messaggero,* asserting with such great eloquence the ridiculous, absurd theory of Agliati's suicide.'

'Now I understand Galbiati's demeanour, and his ironic phrases about Luigi's praise for the article,' exclaimed Giorgio. 'And his zealously obedient acceptance of his chief's enthusiastic remarks!'

The assistant commissioner limited himself to a smile while Bertini continued:

'The article's effect was immediate. The killers were worried because our investigation of the flying boat mystery and of the shooting of Signora Agliati was not going in the direction they had hoped and expected. But they still believed in our mock pretence of total ignorance about everything, Sabelli's murder included. Thus reassured, they thought to solve with one single move every problem to their complete satisfaction. If the police believed in Agliati's suicide and were searching for his dead body on the coast between Ostia and Naples, they would be happy to provide them with the required corpse, to the general and total satisfaction of everybody.'

'But why did they drag the corpse to Pozzuoli Point?'

'Because of a simple question of forensic medicine, my dear Vallesi. After a number of days underwater, a corpse presents a totally different state of decay from another one buried in a garden. Agliati's was in a garden, not in the sea, so they had to leave his body on land, in a very dry place, far away from water and from the coast. Furthermore, it was possible, even after a week, to damage a body in such a way as to give the impression of a fall from the sky. But in its journey, the plane had flown over only one place at a convenient distance from the sea, and that was Pozzuoli Point. So it was quite easy for us to anticipate where they would go. And you can check for yourself how our predictions were correct.'

He pointed out of the restaurant's terrace to the powerful Dilambda in the parking lot, mournfully reflecting its master's disgrace, possibly rejoicing in the excitement of the night's escapade and anticipating all the adventures that fate might have in store for such a magnificent, classy roadster.

A week after, Luigi Renzi visited the Arteni's swanky mansion to present his congratulations for the betrothal of Marcella and Giorgio Vallesi, and, incidentally, hoping to be congratulated for his recent appointment as High Commissioner at the Alba Police Department. The Arteni-Vallesi marriage was fixed for October and the household was duly excited by the nuptial preparations. Vallesi met him at the door, almost transformed by the magic of love as the new Master of the Swanky House. After the foreseeable exchange of congratulations, the obvious object of any conversation was The Great Flying Boat Mystery.

'For you, it was really a great success, my dear Luigi. Every newspaper is praising you for your redoubtable sleuthing skill!'

Luigi's attempt at a humble smile was unsuccessful.

'Ah, I still can't believe how you managed to solve the Vanishing Act Trick. The Double Act was masterfully organized and executed! And I, in the meantime.... '

'You? ' Luigi seemed apparently lost in his humble, self-effacing thoughts.

'I was chasing Agliati's phantom in Mergellina Station, running after a cloaked and muffled and totally innocent fellow from Naples to Rome! A marvellous wild goose chase! Ah, what a blunder! Ah, what an ass I was!'

'Well, it was quite a blunder, I agree, but.... '

'But? ' asked Vallesi in his usual aggressive way.

'You were chasing wild geese, and you caught instead a gorgeous, magnificent butterfly. Next time, I promise, I will follow your example. A splendid butterfly is far better than a disappearing dead banker, I'm afraid. Butterflies can fly. Bankers apparently not,' and he mournfully took a tasty canapé from a silver salver.

THE END

THE ITALIAN MYSTERY NOVEL

The first mystery about the Italian mystery novel is whether it exists as an identifiable genre or whether it is merely a concoction of publishers and newspaper reporters. To be sure, there were many mystery novels written and published in Italian during the thirties, but whether they constituted an original national school is highly arguable. Is there a distinctive Italian style of mystery in the same way there is a distinctive French or Japanese one?

Most Italian writers were not very imaginative: they copied massively from foreigners, and they set their own plots either in a very artificial foreign city—such as London, Paris, Boston, or Rio—or an exceedingly localised Rome or Milan or Palermo, populated by hordes of *macchiette* (colourful indigenous characters). Italy had no interest in fantastic literature (science fiction is even more poorly represented than mystery in our bedevilled local production), and completely missed the great chance offered by the rise of popular fiction in the Nineteenth Century; we never had an Italian Stevenson, or Verne, or Wells, and so we never had our own Poe or Doyle or Gaboriau, even though their works were greatly beloved and reprinted from their first appearance. So authentic Italian mystery fiction essentially started from scratch in the thirties, when Italian publisher Mondadori decided that a bevy of local authors could be added to the foreign ones in its stable. But it was an artificial decision, rather than a natural development of Italian popular literature.

The first such writer, Alessandro Varaldo, wrote no locked room mysteries, and his cases of Ascanio Bonichi, a philosophical policeman who opened the way to many other Italian ancestors of Commander Dalgliesh, do not make easy reading nowadays. Varaldo's work was dominated by the influence of coincidence and chance on the solution of a mystery; he was not a fan of rational deductive reasoning, and his moody, rambling cases were too richly populated by exceedingly colourful Roman characters. Bonichi was a strong believer in hypnotism and mesmerism, so his cases featured a lot of hypnotized murderers or sleepwalking thieves, which are unlikely to satisfy a rational Anglo-Saxon reader.

The second and more famous Italian writer was Augusto De Angelis. His Commissario (Chief Inspector) De Vincenzi was another philosopher, similar to Bonichi, but De Angelis—influenced as he was by Wallace and Van Dine—made him solve more interesting and absorbing cases. De Angelis only skirted the impossible crime in *L'Albergo delle tre rose* (The Hotel of the Three Roses), *Il Mistero delle tre orchidee* (The Mystery of the Three Orchids), and above all *Il Do tragico,* the semi-impossible murder of an opera singer during a radio exhibition (partially based on an Edgar Wallace trick). But his novels are well-written and highly interesting (*Il Mistero do Cinecitta, La Gondola della morte, Il Mistero della vergine, Le Sette picche doppiate* are other remarkable De Vincenzi cases).

Another great writer who never actually used the locked room ploy was Giorgio Scerbanenco, a Russian refugee influenced by Queen and Van Dine. Scerbanenco set his very interesting cases in America and his detective was Arthur Jelling, a Reeder-like archivist in the Boston Police Department. He used the Queenesque negative clue very effectively in *l'Antro dei filosofi,* a very moody and bleak murder story in a very Queenesque eccentric family, possibly related to the Hatters of the Tragedy of Y. Other notable Jelling cases were *La Bambola cieca, Sette giorni di preavviso,* and *Il Cane che parla,* and they are all highly interesting and well-written. As a plotter, Scerbanenco was less amateurish and rambling than De Angelis, and far more orthodox in his use of detection and logical deductions. Later in the Sixties he began a very famous Noir series with unfrocked and disbarred surgeon Duca Lamberti, but these cases are, for me, far more imitative and commonplace than the highly ingenious and original Jelling cases.

The third Italian Grand Master of Mystery again wrote no locked room novels, even if he was very influenced by French mystery literature, and particularly by Leroux and Simenon. Ezio D'Errico was a surrealistic painter and an exponent of the Futurists, tied to the Paris surrealists. His Commissaire Richard was clearly an imitation of Maigret, but his Paris was far more colourful and lively than the bleak, foggy town described by Simenon. D'Errico had the wit to blend other, more fantastic influences with Simenon in his personal cocktail (particularly Leroux and the French Grand-Guignol) and

Richard was confronted by far more picturesque murderers than his Belgian ancestor. In *La Famiglia Morel*, D'Errico invented a very interesting and politically incorrect trick for hiding a highly surprising culprit. In *Il Naso di cartone*, Richard uncovered a very clever motivation for the apparent madness of a serial-killer who put a comical Mardi Gras cardboard nose on his victims. Other highly original and wonderfully well-written Richard cases *were La Scomparsa del defino, La Casa inhabitable,* and *La Donna che ha visto*.

The fourth ace of the Italian Hand was Tito Spagnol, a screenwriter who worked with Frank Capra. Spagnol invented a Van Dinesque detective, Al Gusman, very much like Ellery Queen and having the great distinction of being published in France in the remarkable Gallimard Detective collection before being published in Italy. Again, Gusman solved no impossible cases, but both *L'Unghia del leone* and *La Notte impossible* are highly interesting Italian masterpieces of murder and detection. *La Notte impossible*, for instance, embellished a trick from a Parker Pyne short story by Agatha Christie, developing it into a full-length novel of murder in a closed mansion with a strong Queenian flavour, and using it with the outrageously extreme ingenuity of a Leroux. It's the only use of this very original trick in novel form, to the best of my knowledge, and one can only dream about what could have been made of it by Queen or Christie, if she had made it into a novel instead. In the late Thirties, Spagnol decided to set a more local (and highly praised) detective series, narrating the investigations of a catholic priest named Don Poldo, set in his native Veneto . He was not an Italian Father Brown because his cases lacked the creepy, weird and fantastic metaphysical complexity of GKC: Don Poldo was far nearer to a mild English vicar solving cases in a Miss-Marple-St.Mary Mead-like setting, but in *La Bambola insanguinata* he did solve one of the many classic semi-impossible murders typical of the Italian version of this beautiful subgenre, so unclassifiable for the despairing critic

Thus it was, sad to say, that the locked room puzzle in Italy was the province of less famous and expert authors, and the only book by Franco Vailati, the very novel you have just read, is certainly the best and most original example by an Italian writer.

Another very good deviser of locked room plots was Carlo

Martinelli,a minor author who, after World War II, rewrote his exploits of a French detective named De Galmain and transformed them into the cases of a more American shamus named Mooney (partially inspired again by Ellery Queen):both *l'Impossibile verita* (aka *La Morte chiama nel buio*) and his masterpiece *Il Segreto di una notte* (aka *E Il giorno nuovo spunto*) are well-deserving of attention, particularly the latter with its locked room murders in a closed mansion.

Another minor practitioner of locked room murders was Guglielmo Somalvico, author of technically complex (if a bit improbable) impossible crimes, boldly explained with plans and diagrams—a sort of minor Italian Rupert Penny. *Il Delitto invisibile*, with an impossible murder on a bridge, is easiest to find, but is unfortunately his least-interesting murder story. Far more rewarding are the very rare *Il Microfono sulla tomba* and *La Torcia umana*,with its apparently ubiquitous killer, reminiscent of Noel Vindry's *Le Double alibi* (The Double Alibi)

Magda Cocchia Adami painstakingly explained the mystery of a disappearing van in *Il Furgone fantasma*, famous translator Alfredo Pitta vaguely skirted impossible murder in *Endertone e il delitto impossibile,* and in the creepy but not very impossible *Albergo della paura,* offering to the reader a very surprising murderer and an interesting use of the haunted tree theme, many years before the wonderful and unsurpassed classic of the genre *L'Arbre aux doigts tordus* (The Vampire Tree) by Paul Halter. Alessandro De Stefani used a famous Poe trick quite comically to explain a series of locked cabin shipboard thefts in the humorous *La Crociera del Colorado.* Futurist Luciano Folgore devised a couple of locked room murder spoofs with ludicrous, absurd solutions in *La Trappola colorata* and in the short story *"Il Castello degli echi."* Enzo Gemignani used a murderous room theme for his *La Camera tragica,*one of the many exploits of his Japanese sleuth Yama Koto, a Mister Moto imitation solving cases in Rio de Janeiro. Another Yama Koto case, *Il Gran premio della morte,* can loosely be considered the semi-impossible murder of a prize horse during a grand prix.

Famous songwriter Vasco Mariotti was a very interesting writer of peculiar mystery novels, strongly influenced by Leroux and Maurice Renard. *L'Uomo dai piedi di fauno* is the fantastic, very Leroux-like story of a monstrous serial killer lurking in a grim, creepy and very phony Turin. *La Valle del pianto grigio* is his only locked room, partially based on a famous Conan Doyle trick and using a very Doylesque exotic revenge, using an effective flashback technique. Unfortunately the Pinocchio-like comic con artist-swindler sleuth nicknamed Lo Spennagrulli (the SuckerTrapper) renders this effort quite unpalatable and childish—a strange, uncanny blend of Doyle and Collodi—which is a pity because the melodramatic but sinister plot is not bad at all.

However, a more famous and interesting Italian locked room mystery was not a novel but a stage play by the famous playwright and screenwriter Edoardo Anton. *Il Serpente a sonagli*, the story of a series of impossible murders of young students in a girls'college—only apparently based on the well-worn Speckled Band trick—was later adapted into a famous movie ,with some success.

Italy's catastrophic participation in World War II was the most impossible crime of them all, and it ended with the apocalyptic death of mystery and detection in my misguided country. For too many years the classic mystery was erased from the literary map by fanatical and uninformed critics. For too many years, thousand of adoring readers enjoyed the foreign books under the disapproving eye of dons, newspaper critics and other Arbiter Elegantiarum, unduly praising the tosh written by their own pets, the Italian mystery writers writing the only possible Italian way to murder: the completely unrealistic "realistic" and "regional" novels by utterly uninteresting authors, in many cases now justly forgotten, but condemning the Italian mystery to the localistic Ghetto and to the awful, barren wasteland of Camilleri and Carofiglio which we are still living in today.

As a result, Italian mystery readers were so scared by an Italian name on the cover of a book that they ran away even from good foreign writers with names like Pronzini or Brussolo. (That was also the reason why Steve Carella was called Carell in the Italian version of the 87th Precinct saga, and David Baldacci was called David B. Ford). So it was for too many decades that the locked room murder was laughed about by ignorant writers and critics and used only for epitomizing what the "good writer" was called to destroy in the Mystery genre. For ages, the only impossible murders to which readers had access were the many variants of the trick painstakingly devised by Italian writer Enzo Russo for his teenage mystery series, in which Italy's answer to Nancy Drew, Rossana Da Valle, solved with zest and panache: the impossible disappearance of a schoolgirl on the stairs of her apartment building *(Giusi e'scomparsa)*; the impossible killing of a private zoo owner apparently mangled by his pet tiger (*La Tigre del Bengala*); the impossible kidnapping of an industrialist (*Pasqua a Parigi*); or the disappearance of a whole train (*Il Vagone scomparso*). Russo used the locked room trick again in an adult crime novel, but *Villa Reale Residence* somehow lacked the merry enjoyment of his children's books, and remained a well-written and well-devised effort, but a bit stilted.

Although *Il Nome della rosa* (The Name of the Rose), still our unique mystery masterpiece, contained a locked room murder, Umberto Eco treated the problem superficially and in an off-hand manner. His later venture into the genre, the quite awful *Baudolino*, is now deservedly forgotten. Critics and Christie experts Calcerano and Fiori presented a well-devised locked room murder in the political thriller *L'Uomo di vetro*. Claudia Salvatori used a similar trick in her playful mystery *Mistero a Castel Rundegg*, but the book was more of a game than a sound and solid detective novel.

And so we enter, sadly and disconsolately, into a very dry and dusty new Millennium, which would have been quite hopeless and mournful, had not a few new authors sprung up miraculously (may I say impossibly?) like daisies in the Nullarbor desert. So let me be your Napoleon Bonaparte, the Aborigine guide and scout, and pick for you from our native Ayers Rock the beautiful flowers carefully tended and planted by Giulio Leoni (his *E Trentuno con la morte* presents a splendid locked room murder during the D'Annunzio Escapade in Fiume, and his *La Donna nella luna* inserted a locked studio murder on the set of the famous Fritz Lang and Thea Von Harbou Sci-Fi effort). And Stefano di Marino briefly abandoned the Spy-story intrigue to give us the almost Lovecraftesque exploits of his conjuror sleuth Bas Salieri. *Il Palazzo dalle cinque porte* is one of the best Italian post-war mysteries. Pietro "Piero" Di Palma ,blogger and locked room expert and enthusiast, has found in LRI's *The Realm of the Impossible* his well-deserved international recognition and, with any luck, Enrico Luceri, another hope of Italian New Age of